The Hollow Vale:

The Crumbling Road

The Gurt Wyrms, the Jinglewyrms, and the Winderwyrms of Farfrey

Poetry of the Fabled Gable of Roman Britain

By Alexander Paul Burton

© 2025, 2026 Alexander Paul Burton
All rights reserved.

First Edition – April 2026

Illustrations: Hand drawn by Alexander Paul Burton

Design: Alexander Paul Burton

This is a work of fiction. Names, characters, places, and incidents are either products of the author's imagination or are used fictitiously. While *The Hollow Vale* draws upon real landscapes, linguistic histories, and the fading echoes of Roman Britain, particularly the West Country and Somerset, it is ultimately a myth, not a map.

https://www.alexanderpaulburton.com/the-hollow-vale-wiki

Author's Note

This Fabled Gable now unfolds its part, within the Tharion Cycle, held close to the heart.

The prose and verses you shall read, are through Caelwyn's eyes, a noble creed. Her language echoes times far gone, as translations from Tharionese are drawn. A fictional tongue of Britannia's shore, spoken round 300 A.D., and no more.

All spellings that may seem a touch unwise, and grammar strange before your eyes, are chosen to preserve the ancient way, to translate Tharionese exactly, I say.

The Tharion Cycle and this Vale so deep, are born of fiction, secrets they do keep. Though roots entwine with places truly known, like Somerset's hills and ruins of stone. The tales of heroes and the ancient myth, are imagined fully, held safely with— history becomes a shadow and a glass, a prism where lost longing soon shall pass.

As each new chapter is unveiled, previous versions may be hailed. You're invited to read them at a special, lower price, for this is not a true tale, full of vice. But somewhere in the mists of Somerset so wide, a memory of an older tale does still abide.

Alexander Paul Burton, April 2025

https://www.alexanderpaulburton.com/the-hollow-vale-wiki

Contents

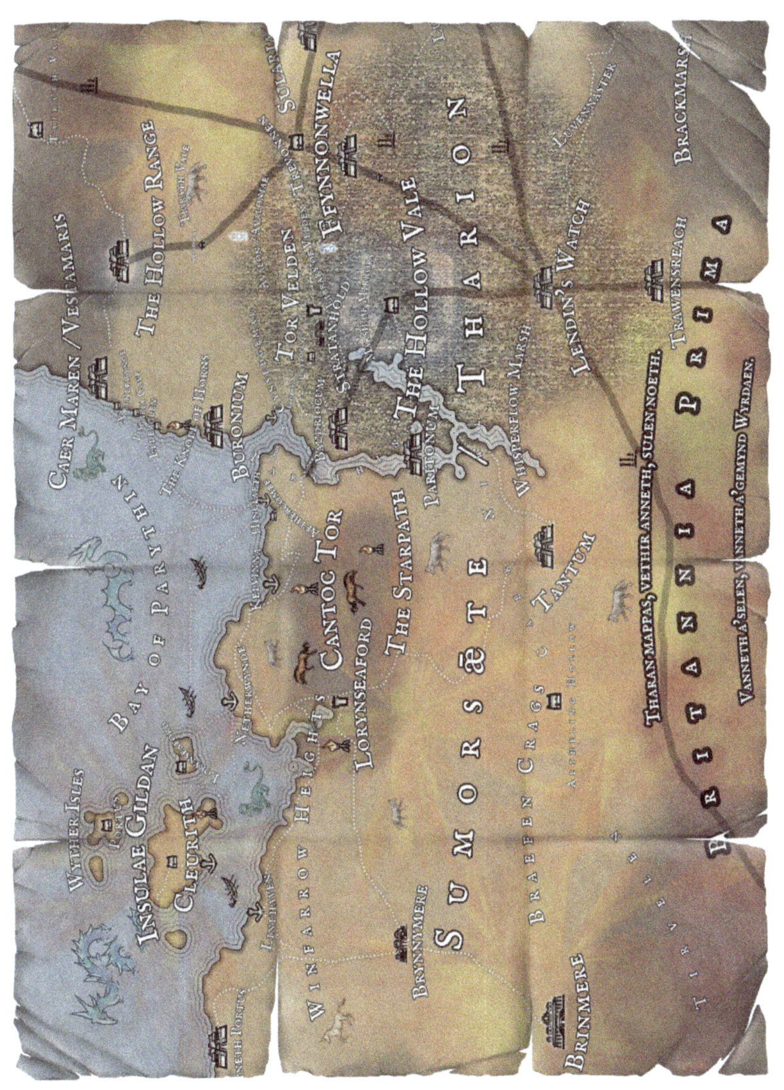

Fantasy Maps of Somerset and Beyond

PISCARIA COVE
ELDERGLEN
THE KNOLL OF HORNS
BURONIUM
RYTH
INNA
HINCLAETH
AETHERCOMBE
C TOR
CYNSEDGEMAR
TOR VE
Northpool / Aetherpool
CATTOCUM
BAUDRIOCUM
STRATANHOLD
LIBRA
MARSH OF MIR
TARPATH
THE HOLLO
PARITONUM
THA
THE
N I W L

THE HOLLOW RANGE
TIARATH VALE
NETHERHOLT
GEMAR
AVALON / AVALONIAE
TOR VELDEN
CUM
TREVONNEN
SULA
LIBRARY OF VELDEN
FFYNNONWELL
TANHOLD
MARSH OF MIRRORS
HOLLOW VALE
HARION

SUMORSÆTE
DRYNARETH
BRINMERE
VELBARITH
CAER PENHUELGOIT
POYNWRENET'S
CAERWEN MYNNAEL
EXMOO
MYNNAION
ISCA DUMNO
NAELPORTUS
SENLORYN
SANTWYR AELWEN
PENWYTH CAELIR
TRETHIRWYN
TORHALLOW
MOUTH OF FFALL
FYTHAEN MORAEL

Chapter I: The Hills Before Rome

Lands ancient on the western-most parts of Britain with fields of green, meadows bright and muddy, heathered hills: this is Somerset, a fogged region of hearty folk, wild wyrms and deep magick. Upon the Quantock Hills there once stood a beacon bright and a small watchtower made of cherrywood; an old station from which the watch-folk could view the small wooden barges float in from yonder shores.

These hills, once known as Cantoc Tor many thousands of years ago, were slowly abandoned over the long years of Roman occupation in Britannia, right up until their departure in the early 400s A.D. It is amongst these hills and small valleys that beasts once roamed. The sandstone, known to reflect great beams of light across the bay, was said to be alive. Its colour, the redness, was said to have been imbued by Caelir The One himself, so as to give the hillside life and its own veins. To this day, the muddy, sodden Quantock Hills still pays homage to this Godly gift.

There was once a great host of many small wyrms who lived amongst the woodland trees, cottage gables and small thatched barns. Wooden houses, and those made of wattle and daub both alike in comfort and warmth. For this is why the wyrms descended on rainy days to the soft woodlands of Pardlestone and the soft, shimmering pebbled beaches of Kilve, known then as Kelvenna. On such days the wild garlic rose from the woodland floor in great heady clouds, and the barge-men of the coast held that to catch that sharp green smell on the air was to know a wyrm had passed. To smell stagnant marsh water on a clear and windless day was to know one was still close.

These wyrms, over many thousands of years, slowly fell asleep. The local folk and barge-men of old knew of them, even before the coming of the Romans and the Great Eagle of imperial might. For when they came, many wyrms were killed or slain. Large beasts, the size of many men, and some smaller, no larger than a hare. These winged beasts sought joy and laughter, not plunder and sadness.

Some of them were brown, or hues of deep red. In their younger years, the wyrms were green in hue and slowly changed to darker shades. Some even grew tired, then fell asleep for years and ended up being covered in a light green moss and dark brown cracks through their skin. They had a merry temperament, though the younger wyrms often grew jealous and haughty. Great fights they would have, even when asleep. Their voices, although dull, could stretch as far as one kilometre on distance; this being an advantage when traversing the great green and brown cliffs of Somerset. It was the younger, haughtier wyrms who were responsible for the missing sheep on the Quantock slopes, and it was they who gave rise to the darker stories. The elder wyrms, those whose scales had deepened into the dark brown of old bracken, disapproved of this strongly.

The female wyrms were wise and true of heart, and though the wyrms did not exhibit gender as we humans do, their happiness was found instead in swimming in fresh-water streams and flying idly through the lichen covered woods and sparse trees of the Quantock Hills.

Truly, a more jovial company of folk one could scarce imagine. Yet the cruel passage of years hath eroded their earthly frames, not with any sudden violence, but with a slow and chilling certainty. Despite their noble nature, they were brought low, destined to be recorded in the dusty scrolls of the past not as a dominant race of wyrms, but as a fractured, melancholy people. The season of grand feasts and the warm glow of hearth-fires beside wyrm-cottages hath vanished; and though we might try to mimic their old gaiety, the Gurt Wyrms are surrendered now to the whims of time and ill-fortune.

They stir only with the first rains of Spring, when the water soaks through the bracken of those unthawed thickets atop the Quantock Hills. Such awakenings occur with a particular urgency in the depths of Shervage Wood, where the Gurt Wyrms remain even unto this hour. They are elusive creatures, oft-times dismissed by the prideful and the blind as nothing more than the twisted roots of an oak or the gnarled bark of a holly tree. The ancient lore of the river-men provides a singular warning: should you stumble upon what seems a fallen timber of immense size, and find it carries the sharp, sweet scent of wild garlic, you would be wise to offer a civil greeting and take your leave with great haste.

Their powerful nature sees their non-binary nature work beautifully, for they are neither on this earth nor entirely of it. They dwell as spiritual compositions between the Physical and Unphysical Hollow Vales, held in a state of entropic superposition. Their true abode, found in the depths of wandering dreams, is a place not entirely to their liking; hence their permanent unquiet across Somerset, the land once known as Tharion.

Their law, a thing both grey with age and sharp with pragmatism, hath been their stay through many hundreds of years. No power of a crown yields their authority; rather, it flows from an ancient covenant of reciprocity and refusal. By this, they transmute the very grain of the world, proffering gifts of change and harvesting only that which may be sustained, as much in spirit as in flesh.

In the time of the river-folk and the old barge-men, they piped tunes of a simple and jovial sort. Though such airs have largely vanished from the world's hearing, they linger yet in the stray melodies we whistle at our idle toil. Little do we know that these half-remembered echoes once possessed the power to make the very earth tremble, for the Winderwyrms would turn their great carmine heads toward the sound, recognising in our breath a thing they had long thought vanished.

The Gurt Wyrm Spindle (Bed-time Chant)

Gurt Wyrm! Gurt Wyrm, Loud and Free!
Under the grey rock,
Appearing as a tree!

Gurt Wyrm! Gurt Wyrm, Carmine and Brown!
Never a sad day,
Never a frown.

Gurt Wyrm! Gurt Wyrm, Time will Change!
In the Hollow Vale,
In the Hollow Range!

Gurt Wyrm! Gurt Wyrm, Long and Green!
Invading Romans,
Hear them scream!

Gurt Wyrm! Gurt Wyrm, Somerset True!
In Shervage Wood,
We'll ark at 'e.

Gurt Wyrm! Gurt Wyrm, Wise and Bold!
We want to sit and listen,
To your tales of old.

Gurt Wyrm! Gurt Wyrm, Living in our Land!
You Westcountry Dragons,
You true fighting band!

Gurt Wyrm! Gurt Wyrm, Loud and Free!
Living amongst us,
Amongst you and me!

*Ark at 'ee or Arketh'ee; meaning Listen to Him or Her

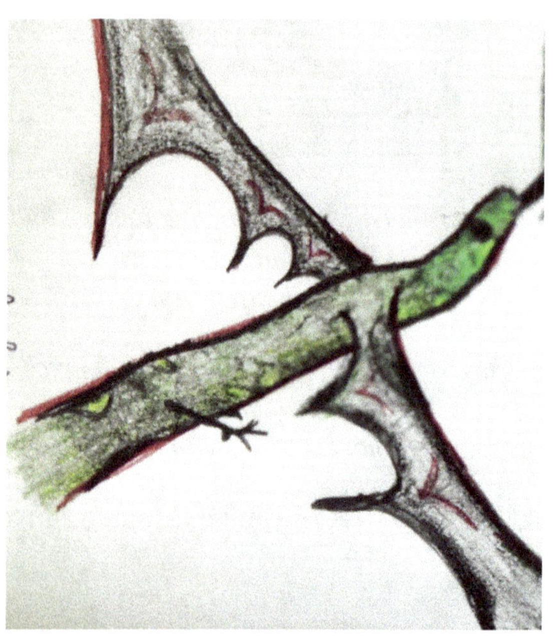

Chapter II: The Jinglewyrms of Snarwood Bay

Long ago these merry Gurt Wyrms learnt new ways on new terrains that tested them in different ways. They no longer were confined to the woodland areas and Shervage Wood but spread north to Kilve and the small beaches, coves and hidden areas all along the coast.

These new wyrm-types, closely related to Gurt Wyrms, preferred the liminal space where the land meets the sea and where the fresh water of the land mingles with the ancient salty sea. For salt is what they craved, whether it be a chalice full of seawater or the salty breeze of residue brought in on the early winds blowing southerly inland.

They emerged, it was said, from the fossil beds themselves, born of the layered red silt that the Quantock

Hills shed each season into the bay. Their scales were not the deep carmine or moss-brown of their Gurt Wyrm cousins but instead shimmered in copper and silver, a kind of living mail that jingled softly as they moved, like Roman denarii dropped into a hollow bowl. It was this sound that gave them their name. The Jinglewyrms of Snarwood Bay were creatures of the fringe, the liminal folk, and they wore this nature like armour.

Their voices differed too from the deep sounds of the Gurt Wyrm which emanated in loud 'cracks'. The Jinglewyrms rang clear and sharp across the water, travelling great distances across the Somerset levels. On still nights their calls carried far out to Wales and often confused the barge-men who mistook them for the harbour bells of Buronium, the very same that guided them toward the port safely at night. Where the Gurt Wyrms sang riddles and rhymes into the darkness of the night, the Jinglewyrms proclaimed the same poems into the light of day and newness of life.

It was the light they loved best. They were drawn to surfaces that caught it and reflected it back with certainty: polished bronze, neat coils of rope, amphorae stacked in rows. When Roman merchant galleys began anchoring in the bay, the Jinglewyrms surfaced at night to admire the tidiness of it all. The order. The definition. The sense that everything had been given a name and a place and a purpose. They had been searching, without knowing they were searching, for something exactly like this.

Deep in the Mendip Hills, not far from the Quantock country, the Romans had discovered lead and silver ore in quantities that made their surveyors giddy. The Mendip mines became one of the most productive operations in all of Britannia.

Some of the older barge-men believed the Jinglewyrms were not merely attracted to Roman silver but were in some sense made of it: spirits of the ore-seams given wing and voice by the disturbance of mining. Whether or not this was true, the Jinglewyrms were undeniably restless from the moment the first Mendip shaft was sunk, and their copper scales took on a new brightness, as if answering a signal from underground.

Slowly, almost imperceptibly, the Jinglewyrms developed a craving for boundaries. They wanted to know where the sea ended and where they began. They wanted names that stayed the same from sunrise to sunset. They began to learn Latin terms for themselves: Serpens Argenteus, the Silver Serpent.

They began, in their whispered conversations at the tide line, to look at the Gurt Wyrms' fluidity as a flaw, a failure to achieve proper form. They whispered that the Gurt Wyrms were confused, unnatural, unable to be pinned to parchment in ink. They framed their cousins' sacred ambiguity as a chaos that needed the order of what they called the Gable: the pitched roof of civilisation that divides the world into neat, knowable halves.

The two kindreds stopped singing together. The Gurt Wyrms retreated further into the deep woods. The Jinglewyrms coiled on sun-warmed stones and practised the grammar of empire, learning to think in the categories the Romans had brought with them: land and sea, civilised and wild, fixed and formless.

They saw in Roman culture a reflection they had been searching for, a world where everything had its place and function, with a name stamped in bronze. What they did not yet see was that this mirror was also a cage.

The Jinglewyrm's Shore Song

Where fresh-water meets the salt of sea,
The Jinglewyrm of Snarwood came,
In copper scales and silver flame,
A jingling, liminal folk set free.

From fossil beds they rose up bright,
Along the bay at Kilve they shone,
And loved the boundary, and the stone,
The Roman galleys' ordered light.

Where Gurt Wyrm sang in questions low,
The Jinglewyrm proclaimed and rang,
A clear, bell-certain, copper clang
Across the water's evening glow.

They loved the neat-stacked amphorae,
The measured rope, the polished prow,
The ledger and the Latin vow,
The named and tidy, day by day.

They called the Gurt Wyrm's nature strange,
Their fluency a flaw, not grace,
Too wide, too wild, no settled place,
Too large for any Roman range.

And so they learnt the Empire's tongue,
Serpens Argenteus, their new name,
And did not see the mirror's game
Was cage enough, for old and young.

Chapter III: The Winderwyrms of Farfrey

On the Origins of the Winderwyrms and Their Ancient Kin

The Winderwyrms were, by blood and ancient covenant, close kin to the Gurt Wyrms of Shervage Wood, though smaller in stature and considerably more restless in temperament. Where the Gurt Wyrms slept their long and mossy sleeps, the Winderwyrms seldom rested for long. Over many thousands of years, they slowly fell into long wandering rather than slumber. Long before the standard of the Great Eagle cast its shadow across the land, the river-folk and those who toiled upon the ancient barges spoke of these creatures in hushed, familiar tones. Yet with the Roman onset came a season of blood; the old ways were trampled, and the Winderwyrms were either put to the sword or forced into a bitter exile from their ancestral tracks.

In the flush of youth, they wore a vibrant, leaf-like verdancy, though the passing of centuries saw their scales deepen into the scorched tones of rusted iron or a bruised, wintry plum. There were those amongst them who, overcome by the weight of their travels, would sink into the damp earth to seek a fleeting respite. These weary wanderers became as one with the hills, their hides mapped with dark, earthen fissures and cloaked in a velvet shroud of emerald moss.

A bright, merry spirit generally governed them, yet the fledglings were prone to fits of vanity and sharp-clawed envy. In their pride, they would fall to bickering, their skirmishes playing out in the high air above the ridges. Whilst they lacked the profound, earth-shaking thunder of the Gurt Wyrm lineage, their cries possessed a piercing clarity that could carry for a full kilometre, a singular boon for those navigating the sheer, bracken-cloaked precipices of Somerset.

The females of the race were noted for a singular steadfastness of spirit. Though their understanding of gender bore little resemblance to the rigid categories of man, they took their greatest delight in the cool embrace of mountain brooks or in drifting, untethered, through the silver-lichened groves and the lonely, wind-swept timber of the Quantock Hills.

Hark! Hark! Hear their song: such a merry bunch of folk they were. Alas, times have worn away their corporeal flesh with no intensity, only inevitability. Even in their virtue they were sullied, to one day be sent into the great annals of history not as a master wyrm-race, but a sad folk, scattered and divided. The days of large banquets and small fires around Winderwyrm-cottages have gone, and though we may seek to emulate them in our own happy way, the Winderwyrms are lost to time and happenstance.

At the first fall of Spring-time, when raindrops pierce deep the bracken of those unthawed woodlands atop the Quantock Hills, they may awaken. Harder still to find than the Gurt Wyrms, these Winderwyrms are oft-times mistaken by the eager and the arrogant for the mere huffing of wind through old holly or the creaking of ancient oak. Theirs is a power that sees their non-binary nature work beautifully, for they are neither on this earth nor entirely of it. They dwell as spiritual compositions between the Physical and Unphysical Hollow Vales in entropic superposition. This deep-wandering is a state not entirely to their liking, hence their permanent unquiet across Somerset, once known as Tharion. Mark how they differ from the Gurt Wyrms: they settle not, they moss not, nor do they sink into the comfortable dark of long sleep. They wander. They seek. They return.

Their law, a thing both grey with age and sharp with pragmatism, hath been their stay through many hundreds of years. No power of a crown yields their authority; rather, it flows from an ancient covenant of reciprocity and refusal. By this, they transmute the very grain of the world, proffering gifts of change and harvesting only that which may be sustained, as much in spirit as in flesh.

In days of yon, they piped tunes of a simple and jovial sort. Though such airs have largely vanished from the world's hearing, they linger yet in the stray melodies we whistle at our idle toil. Little do we know that these half-remembered echoes once possessed the power to make the very earth tremble, or caused a Winderwyrm to turn its great carmine head toward the sound, recognising in our breath a thing they had long thought vanished.

Now, attend! For here the tale grows passing strange. These wyrms did not pace only the muddy hills and lichen-cloaked vales of Somerset. Their flitting between the Vales—that restless superposition of being—granted them passage to lands quite wiped from human cartography. These are shores that sit between the collapse of one moral waveform and the lifting of the next, places that exist in their fullness only when the eye finds them. One such land was Farfrey; and here follows what the Winderwyrms found therein, what Farfrey taught them, and what neither hath since forgotten.

The Winderwyrm's Road

The Gurt Wyrm sleeps in Shervage deep,
In moss and root and sandstone's red,
But Winderwyrm will never keep
To any single hill or bed.

They wander where the waveforms fall,
Between the Vales of flesh and dream,
Not wholly answering any call,
Not always wholly what they seem.

In early Spring the bracken stirs,
A carmine wing disturbs the air,
The old oak creaks, the holly blurs,
And something ancient passes there.

Their covenant is this alone:
To take what's needed, nothing more,

To give what's good, to leave the stone
As living as it was before.

And when the hills of Somerset
Grow too familiar and too still,
The Winderwyrm has not left yet,
Only wandered to the next hill.

For they will find, between the rain
And the bracken and the morning grey,
A land no map has ever lain,
And go there, and observe, and stay.

Interlude: The Land of Farfrey and the Great Muffin Reckoning

Being a True Account of Quantum Ethics, Moral Baking, and the Snarleygogs of Grumblesome Hill

In the Land of Farfrey, where the Wumble trees grew in shades that had no name in Somerset and the sky ran a deep and unapologetic orange above grass of an equally improbable blue, the air was so thick you could chew it like cheese and the heat so heavy it pressed on the shoulders like a patient and extremely warm obligation. Nothing in Farfrey was quite what it seemed, which suited the Winderwyrms very well indeed.

There lived in Farfrey certain beings who were, by general agreement, enormous and grand. Their hands were like great boulders and their Winderwyrms were so mighty they sat right on their shoulders, which they swung through the heat of Farfrey with a flair that bordered on the theatrical. The Zibbles whispered about them. The Plonks confirmed it. The Wumble-tree mayors had no authority over them, and the Splonkish High Court had tried once and preferred not to discuss it. The Winderwyrms ran Farfrey of a quite different sort, and they were large enough about it to flick their mighty Winderwyrms with an air that said the heat of Farfrey was entirely their doing, which the Wibbles and the Ploops believed entirely, melting as they did like Farfrey's finest warm soups.

Over yonder, however, on Grumblesome Hill, where the Farfrey wind stopped and the whole world held its breath, there lurked the Snarleygogs. They were lumpy, they were loud, their great gnarly noses were perpetually elevated into the nearest available cloud, and they had seventeen chins apiece, which gave their grumbling a remarkable range and depth. They hated the Winderwyrms with a thoroughness that would have been admirable if applied to almost anything else. Their complaint was simple: that the Winderwyrms had marvellous things, and the Snarleygogs also had marvellous things, things gnarly and great, and that the heat of Farfrey ought by rights to have been their domain also.

Here is where Farfrey grew curious and odd, and where the Somerset Winderwyrms, newly arrived on their great carmine wings, became relevant. For when they landed, they found that nobody had yet made any choice at all. The Winderwyrms had not swung. The Snarleygogs had not baked. The whole of great Farfrey sat in a superposition, a state of not-yet, of neither decided nor collapsed nor set, like

Schrodinger's cat before anyone thought to look. Nothing in Farfrey had fully resolved. No moral question had quite been dissolved. The Winderwyrms from Somerset understood this immediately and settled in to observe, because observing was what they did best and because the kitchen of Farfrey smelled extremely interesting.

Before the first muffin was baked, Farfrey existed in a state of pure potential. This is the quantum ethical truth of all beginnings: no moral outcome exists until the waveform collapses, until a choice is made, an action taken, a muffin placed inside an oven.

Now the Winderwyrms of Farfrey had one guilty pleasure beyond the swinging of Winderwyrms and the flicking of heat, and that was the baking of muffins. Their kitchen was massive, fitted with Winderwyrm-sized spatulas, bowls of considerable circumference, ovens large enough to warm a modest moon, and measuring cups shaped like each Winderwyrm's spoon. The biggest Winderwyrm, whose name was Grosse and who carried himself with the authority of someone who has been the biggest Winderwyrm for a very long time, announced one day that they would bake the Great Muffin, the muffin most close to perfection, to beauty, to moral excellence, a muffin so righteous it practically shone. The Zibbles pressed their noses against the warm glass and the Plonks struck poses of eager attention.

The Somerset Winderwyrms settled along the high sill with their carmine wings folded and their old bodies still, for they too had come to observe and to learn.

Grosse reached for the flour, and here was the moment, the singularity, the zero at the bottom of the letter V, the point before free: the choice unresolved, the batter not mixed, the muffin not yet true. He stood at the place where the two branches split. The right branch required patience, correct measurement, butter worked low, eggs folded gently, batter set right. The left branch was easy: too much sugar, too fast, frosting piled in, quick and sweet and immediately wrong, the easy-path muffin, the popular song.

A Zibble cried out that the easy muffin rose fast and was golden and covered in dribble and the most popular muffin in all of the town. Grosse held his Winderwyrm steady and replied that they should wait. He slid the fast muffin into the oven and it rose in an instant to a glorious dome and the Plonks oohed and aahed with genuine feeling.

The eldest Somerset Winderwyrm tilted her ancient head. She had seen this before, not in Farfrey but in the red sandstone hills of Cantoc Tor, in the long Roman years, when the fast-built and easy was greeted with cheers and then abandoned and then crumbled and then covered in moss and then forgotten entirely at considerable loss.

The fast muffin wobbled. It sagged in a haze. It sank in the middle, it puckered and fell, and it smelt considerably less of muffin and considerably more of something else.

The quick muffin, Grosse said, completely composed, had collapsed exactly as the waveform supposed. The fast-risen choice always falls in the end, for evil's own value will always descend.

The eldest Winderwyrm made a sound, low and warm, not quite a word but something that filled the room entirely. In Somerset once, she said, when the Zibbles looked up, they had learnt this at considerable personal cost. The Romans built fast with their roads and their stone, and the Quantock Hills outlasted each one. They watched and they waited. They always do. The slow thing is truer. The slow thing comes through.

The fast muffin is the ethical choice made in haste, under pressure, for immediate reward. Its value at the point of rising is real but uncollapsed in a moral sense. When the waveform finally settles and the true nature of the muffin is revealed, its value is always half of what it appeared. The Winderwyrms, who had spent several thousand years in entropic superposition between two Hollow Vales, could have told anyone this at any point. Nobody had thought to ask them.

On Grumblesome Hill, through the Wumble tree thicket, the Snarleygogs heard about the Winderwyrms' great biscuit. They called it a biscuit because the Snarleygogs believed muffins and biscuits to be the same thing, which they are not, and which is perhaps the earliest sign of trouble.

They tumbled and stumbled into their grey kitchen with their gnarly great hands in a state of considerable bad temper and grabbed all the flour and dumped it in fast. They added the sugar in an avalanche, then seventeen eggs, then some butter, then spite. Yes, spite, for the Snarleygog recipe called for two cups of grudge and a generous measure of bitterness, and their leader read from his scroll that if you added just a cupful of someone else's blame, the muffin would rise faster and taste just the same.

A younger Winderwyrm, green-hued still and new, had followed the Snarleygogs through the Wumble-tree thicket and peered through the kitchen glass with the expression of someone who has seen spite in kitchens before. In the long Roman years of Britannia's shore, she had watched legions build what they would later ignore: fast walls, fast decisions, fast bridges, fast pride, and then, inevitably, the collapsing inside.

The Zibbles who had wandered from the main gathering said oh dear and oh my in succession and noted that resentment had been added, and also some bother.

The Snarleygog muffin went into the oven and rose like a monument grand, the tallest great muffin in all Farfrey's land, and the Snarleygogs whooped and paraded and twirled, which was a difficult feat for beings that gnarled, and declared that they had beaten the great Winderwyrms, that their muffin was best, that it had passed every test.

The eldest Zibble, who was uncommonly wise in the way that those who have watched a great many waveforms collapse become uncommonly wise, said only: wait. Just wait. Give it time. The waveform's not settled. It's yet to decline.

And slowly, so slowly, the muffin came down. The tallest great muffin became the most brown, then the most slightly burnt, then the most slightly grey, then the most slightly inedible, then thrown away.

The Snarleygogs roared that this was impossible, that they had followed their recipe with care, used all their grudges and all their spite, and could not understand why their great muffin had turned out not right.

The eldest Zibble stepped forward and spoke with a voice like a bell wrapped in warm Farfrey smoke. The Snarleygog muffin had been the quick-option choice of the moral debris: it rose without effort, looked rather fair, but the value it held was only ever half there. The muffin baked quickly with bitterness in would always, in time, be a collapsed waveform sin. The Winderwyrms baked slowly, their muffin took care, their muffin took longer, but their muffin stayed there.

The green Winderwyrm flew back through the rain to settle beside the eldest and said only this, in the tongue of the old wyrm-blood thread: they reminded her of the young ones, before, when the Winderwyrms fought over hillsides and asked what things were for, when they thought the fastest and loudest would win, before they learnt patience, before they grew in.

The eldest Winderwyrm said nothing for a long while. Then she made that same sound again, low and mild, not quite agreement, not quite consolation, something more ancient: the sound of observation.

The Snarleygog muffin demonstrates a key principle of quantum ethics: evil or ugliness, as a moral choice, achieves initial value quickly. Its waveform collapses almost immediately into an impressive but ultimately unstable form. The value of the Snarleygog Muffin at its peak is, by quantum ethical law, exactly half the value of the Winderwyrm Muffin at its peak. This is not a punishment. It is simply mathematics.

Word spread quickly through Farfrey-at-large that a bake-off was coming, a contest of charge, and that the Winderwyrms and Snarleygogs each held a claim to the greatest great muffin and the glory of fame. The Zibbles set up an enormous table at the centre of Farfrey, near old Wumble's Stable, and every last creature in Farfrey turned out: the Ploops, the Wibbles, the Snorfs with their snout. The Somerset Winderwyrms settled along the old wall with their carmine wings folded, not judges, not bakers, not tellers of fate, but observers, which mattered considerably.

Even your narrator came wandering through, wiping sweat from the brow in the Farfrey-ish blue, from the corner of Brimble and Squee, to observe the great baking and soak up the sun.

The eldest Zibble announced the rules: each baker must choose how they make their great batch, and the moral observer would carefully watch. Observing, as she explained, is the whole point of things. The quantum collapse of all muffins and kings depends not just on the baker alone but on those who observe what the baker has shown. The K-value, the efficiency score of all those who watch and reflect and explore the moral dimensions of baking and taste, decides how much value is given in haste.

The Winderwyrms understood this in their ancient bones. Their covenant of reciprocity, inscribed not in stones but in the living superposition between the two Hollow Vales, had always held that the observer's own part in collapsing the waveform is a moral art. To watch well is to add to the goodness accrued. To watch poorly is to leave the whole thing unreviewed.

The Snarleygogs scoffed that their muffin needed nobody's eyes and barrelled back into their kitchen. The Winderwyrms said nothing. They nodded and, slow, began mixing their batter with patience and flow. They measured each cup with a Winderwyrm-sized care. They folded the eggs with a thoroughness rare. The Snarleygogs, halfway through, announced that they had practically won.

The crowd leaned and watched, and the watching was key. The Snarleygog muffins came out golden and risen and perfectly round and were the most beautiful muffins that anyone found for exactly thirty-two seconds before they fell, concave in the middle, with a rather bad smell, the grudge and the spite now exposed to the air turning the beautiful muffins to something less fair.

The Winderwyrms' came out. Not as tall. Not as grand. But perfect in measure, each one fully planned. They held their round tops and kept their warm smell and were muffins of substance that nobody could fell.

The crowd tasted both. The Snarleygog muffin was sweet for one blinding instant, then ashy and complete. The Winderwyrm muffin was slower to fill up the tongue but the flavour, once settled, rang out like a song.

The eldest Winderwyrm ate neither. She simply sat and observed the whole room with the quiet of that ancient practice, the one from the Quantock Hills grey, of watching the outcome without having your say. Then she made the sound again, and this time it carried. Every creature in Farfrey heard it and tarried. It was not words. It was older than words. It was the sound of something that has waited long enough and found, without triumph or grief, without envy or spite, that the slow thing was true and the true thing was right.

The crowd cried that the Winderwyrms had won through, that the slow muffin was the right muffin, the muffin that was true. The Snarleygogs spluttered and argued and roared, but even the Snarleygogs, deep down, were floored.

The crowd who watched the baking were not passive. Their observation, their collective moral attention, contributed to the efficiency, or K-value, of the final outcome. A muffin baked in private, unobserved, still collapses its waveform, but the aggregate of moral observation accelerates the recognition of true value. The Winderwyrms understood this from long practice. Their K-value, accrued across centuries of patient watching from the lichen-covered hills of Somerset, was considerable. And Farfrey felt it.

Now here is the part that the Zibbles had saved, the part that the Ploops had most anxiously craved, the part where old Farfrey received its full answer to why the slow muffin outlasted the dancer.

The eldest Zibble, who had seventeen fewer chins than the Snarleygogs and considerably more wisdom per chin, stood up on the table and addressed Farfrey thus. She told them that the lesson of muffins was not who had won but the shape of all muffins beneath the same sun. If they added up the goodness of every great batch the Winderwyrms had baked since the very first catch of Farfrey-flour mixed in the great Farfrey bowl, the sum of that goodness would accumulate whole. It grows and it grows, slowly, yes, but it grows, while evil's own sum shrinks wherever it goes, for the Snarleygog total, however they try, will always be half of the Winderwyrms' great pile.

This is the Omega: the sum of all sums, the aggregate goodness that endlessly comes. For evil collapses to half in the end, a shadow of goodness forever to bend. Every muffin baked every day is a choice at the bottom of V, and the right branch is slower than the wrong one but it is the right branch, and the wet muffin drowns you in sugar and sin while the dry muffin's patient and the dry muffin wins. And the one who observes it, who watches with care, adds their K-value into the beautiful air.

The eldest Winderwyrm rose from the wall. She was old enough to remember before the fall of the Roman roads, before the long sleep began, before the first Winderwyrm had learnt what it means to live in superposition between what the world is and what it has always been. She spoke not in rhyme, for the Winderwyrms never did. She spoke in the old way, the Somerset way, of plain words and long pauses and things simply said, the way the Quantock Hills speak in the early grey thread of morning before the bracken has woken.

We have been in the superposition for a very long time, she said. We did not know when we would arrive at our own Omega. We knew only that the wandering was the thing, and the watching was the thing, and the not-choosing-quickly was the thing. The Hollow Vale between our two states of being was not a punishment. It was a patience. And patience, given long enough, becomes something that even mathematics must eventually respect.

The Winderwyrms stood still. The Snarleygogs shuffled and their grumbling ceased. The youngest Snarleygog, with only nine chins, asked quietly whether they could learn how the right baking begins.

The Winderwyrms looked over. A long pause. Then: yes, they said, because goodness just does. It doesn't need enemies. Doesn't need foes. It measures. It folds. And patiently grows.

The eldest Winderwyrm settled her wings and said nothing further. She had said enough. It was enough.

So they baked, all together, the one final muffin: the Winderwyrms, the Snarleygogs, the Zibbles still huffing with joy rather than fury, the Ploops, the Wibbles, the Snorfs and the Farfrey-folk dear. The Somerset Winderwyrms watched from the wall, their carmine and green-hued kin attending it all, adding their K-value, ancient and earned, to the aggregate goodness so patiently learned. They measured the flour in a shared careful cup, folded the batter together with heads up, placed it with patience inside the great oven and nobody argued and nobody shoved and it rose. Slowly. Perfectly. True.

The most glorious muffin that Farfrey ever knew. Not tall as the Snarleygogs' quick-risen pride, not flashy, not instant, not puffed out too wide, but golden and steady and fully there, with a smell that said goodness and a warmth beyond fair.

Your narrator, still on the corner of Brimble Street and Squee, took a bite. If muffins could tell you the meaning of right, this one would have told of patience and choice, of the V and its branches, of the Zibble's calm voice, of the Omega sum where all goodness arrives, of the Winderwyrms' dignified and carmine-winged lives, and of something else too, something older and wide, a thing that had flown across Somerset's tide and arrived in this orange and blue-grassed land to observe and be patient and quietly stand.

Perhaps, your narrator said, mopping the crumbs from the chin, the whole thing was never about who would win. Perhaps it was always about how we bake, what we choose to put in for each other's sake.

The Snarleygogs nodded their seventeen chins. And Farfrey glowed warm where the slow goodness begins.

The Winderwyrms rose on their great carmine wings, circled once over Farfrey and all of its things, and flew back toward Somerset, back to the hills, back to the bracken and lichen and morning-damp stills of Shervage Wood and the Quantock Hills wide, where their Gurt Wyrm cousins still sleep in the side of the ancient red sandstone that Caelir made bright. They did not say farewell. Winderwyrms never quite do. They left only the melody, low and simple and true, the tune we all whistle when working alone, not knowing it once made the earth tremble and moan, not knowing it carried a message from lands where the sky was quite orange and the muffin demands everything patient and good from the one who will bake it, and everything honest from those who will make it.

And the heat? Well. The heat was just fine. It always is, when the right muffin is shared.

The final muffin of Farfrey is not the product of one great baker or one dominant force. It is the product of the aggregate: the sum of all moral choices, all careful measurements, all patient folding and slow rising. This is the Omega: not a point of ending but of accumulation. Evil, as the Snarleygog method proved, can never reach it. Its value will always be half. But goodness, slow as marble rather than fast as plaster, endures. It outlasts the heat. It outlasts the grumbling. The Winderwyrms, who had waited in entropic superposition between the Hollow Vales for longer than Farfrey had existed, understood the Omega not as a formula but as a lived thing: a thing you arrive at not by rushing but by continuing.

Chapter IV: Rome at the Shore

By 400 CE the Roman legions were stretched thin across a dwindling empire, their cultural shadow lying long and dark across Somerset even as the edifice itself began to tremble. Governors still ruled from Aquae Sulis, that great bath-city of stone, still demanding tribute, still dreaming of eternal order as Britannia slipped from the imperial grasp like wet clay between closing fingers.

The Jinglewyrms allied with the governors in those final years, trading ancient secrets for Roman titles and protection. They revealed sacred springs, hidden ore veins, pathways through the marshes that had been kept only in wyrm-memory for a thousand years. In return they were granted the hollow title of Custodes Litoris, Guardians of the Coast, and they wore this designation like armour, polishing it daily the way they polished their copper scales.

The landscape was being cut by the strata, the straight roads that drove like spears through the yielding earth. The Fosse Way split the Somerset countryside with an arrogance that the Gurt Wyrms found obscene. To them, roads were iron shackles pinning the shifting earth into permanent, predictable shapes. Every milestone was a declaration: Here. Not there. This. Not that. The Romans measured everything. They counted trees in Shervage Wood for timber, assessed streams for mills, surveyed hills for fortifications, reduced the living world to resource and record.

The Jinglewyrms assisted in all of this, believing with sincere and tragic conviction that they were helping to bring enlightenment. The Gurt Wyrms watched from the shadows of the deep wood and grieved not in anger but in the way that old things grieve: quietly, slowly, the way moss grows over what has been lost.

The Roman Augur and the Great Log of Shervage

There is a story, not recorded in any Roman document because Roman documents do not record the things that made their writers feel foolish, of an Augur named Decimus who was sent to survey the timber potential of Shervage Wood in the third century A.D. He came with surveyors, a tablet of wax, and the absolute conviction that he could count and categorise anything he encountered. He entered the wood on a morning in late October, when the wild garlic had faded but still left its ghost in the damp air, a sharp green smell that the surveyors found unsettling. The wood was very quiet. Not the quiet of emptiness but the quiet of attention.

He came upon what appeared to be a very large fallen oak, moss-covered and ancient. He calculated board feet. He assigned it a category in his wax tablet: Materia, category three, suitable for shipbuilding. He was about to move on when one of the junior surveyors, a young man from Gaul who had only arrived in Britannia the previous spring, said quietly: 'Sir. I think it breathed.'

Decimus looked at him with the expression of a person who has spent thirty years learning to see only what is useful. 'Timber,' he said, 'does not breathe.'

He wrote his category and moved on. The young Gaul said nothing further. He had seen the moss move. He never ate wild garlic again for the rest of his life. In his retirement in Lugdunum, on certain autumn mornings, he would wake from dreams of a wood that was watching him with a patience so profound it made the entire Roman Empire feel like a brief afternoon.

The Centurion who later brought his surveyors' chains to the eastern edge of the wood, seeking to lay a road through the heart of the Wyrm-sleep, saw only an obstacle to the Emperor's straight line. The road was never built. The Fosse Way went round.

The Watcher's Poem

The road came straight as Roman will,
Through fen and spring and ancient way,
It speared the wood and topped the hill
And named the living world its clay.

Here. Not there. This. Not that.
The milestone drove into the sod.
The Jinglewyrm coiled, glossy-flat,
And called the milestone-maker God.

They gave the springs, the hidden ore,
The marsh-paths only wyrm-blood knew,

And wore the title Custodes lore
As if a name could make things true.

The Gurt Wyrm watched from Shervage deep,
As ley-lines bent to straight-cut stone,
And could not rouse itself from sleep
Enough to mourn what it had known.

For grief in wyrm-time is not fast,
It grows like moss on what is gone,
The slow, the quiet, the steadfast
Keep mourning after hope moves on.

Chapter V: The Charge of Betrayal

From the hollows of Shervage, the Gurt Wyrms issued their silent, thunderous decree, rippling it through root and stone across all of Somerset. The alliance between the Jinglewyrms and the Romans was, in the eyes of the Gurt Wyrm covenant, a Betrayal of the Pact. It was an ancient understanding, older than the hills themselves and considerably older than any road the Romans had ever cut through them, that the land belongs to itself and not to those who merely walk upon it.

The Jinglewyrms had traded the richness of their being for the comfort of definition. They had sold their birthright for the warm, shallow pleasure of knowing their place. Rome was depicted by the Gurt Wyrms in their deep, tectonic song as a force that eats the world by naming it. Every Latin word laid upon a living thing was a small death: taking the breathing, shifting mystery of existence and reducing it to a term in a ledger. By joining this enterprise, the Jinglewyrms had become part of the machine that consumes the wild, that turns forest into timber resource and sacred spring into aquifer.

The Gurt Wyrms sent an emissary, an ancient one, half-oak and half-serpent, who moved through the woodland as slowly as the centuries themselves. The message was simple: renounce Rome, or be renounced by the land itself. The Jinglewyrms, draped in their Roman titles, scales polished to mirror brightness, refused.

They had forgotten how to hear the language of the threshold. Even as the Gurt Wyrms prepared for what must come, they were keen for the days when all wyrms had moved as one, when the distinction between hill and shore was merely geographic and not philosophical. They mourned the future that could now never be.

The Decree

Renounce them now, the tectonic said,
Through root and silt and ancient clay,
The land belongs not to the dead
Nor those who only pass this way.

To sell the spring, to name the wood,
To tell the Roman where the ores run,
Is not enlightenment or good:
It is the thing already done.

The Jinglewyrm in copper-bright
Had learnt so well the Empire's tongue
It could not hear the ancient right,
The law it knew when it was young.

Come back, come back, the decree rang,
Through Quantock stone and Kilve's shore,
But bright the Jinglewyrm's armour sang
And bright it stayed, and nothing more.

So mourn the song that once rang true,
The hill and shore in common breath,
The Gurt Wyrm mourned the old, the new,
And then prepared the thing like death.

Chapter VI: The Slaying of the Jinglewyrms

The Gurt Wyrms descended from the ridgeway like a landslide given consciousness. It was not the movement of a fighting force but something older and more inevitable than that: the movement of the land itself, reasserting its nature. The collision was not between equals but between mountain and metal, between the ancient stone of Somerset and the imported order of empire.

The bells of the Jinglewyrms rang out in alarm, then confusion, and then with a terrible, crystalline shattering were silenced by the crushing weight of the hills. They were buried in red silt that would, centuries later, be mistaken by quarrymen for simple sediment and nothing more. The Gurt Wyrms did not fight as Romans fought. They formed no lines, followed no commands, sought no glory and declared no victory. They moved as water moves, as roots move, with an inevitability that has no need for drama. They did not kill with tooth or claw but by being more fundamentally real than the Jinglewyrms' borrowed certainty could withstand.

This was not a triumph. The Gurt Wyrms themselves understood it as a grim pruning, the sorrowful cutting away of an infected branch to save the greater tree. They wept as they did it, their great tectonic voices carrying the grief of it across every root from the Quantock Hills to Exmoor. They mourned the loss of the bell-song even as they knew that the bell-song had become a poison, a vector for the empire's reality-consuming logic. The bells they silenced had once been beautiful. That was the tragedy of it.

When the tide returned and washed over the shore where the Jinglewyrms had coiled, the copper and silver had gone dull, oxidised by salt and sorrow. The Jinglewyrms were not destroyed but unmade, returned to the formlessness they had once feared above all things. Their desperate grasp at fixed identity was finally loosened. For three days and three nights no bird sang on the Somerset coast. The land itself observed a period of grief for what might have been, for the future where wyrms of hill and shore might have found a way to honour both fluidity and form without destroying either.

The Musical March Song

They came as water comes in flood,
As roots push upward through the clay,
Not rage, not glory, only blood
Of kinship cut and mourned away.

No line was drawn, no war-cry made,
No banner raised above the slain,

Only the necessary trade
Of what must pass for what remains.

The bells rang bright in copper-clear
Then cracked in salt and sorrow's weight,
The hill came down with neither fear
Nor triumph, only being's freight.

They wept, the Gurt Wyrms, as they cut
The branch that had become a bane,
The bell-song beautiful and shut
Would never ring the shore again.

Three days no bird sang Kilve's long beach,
The land kept grief the only way
A land can keep it, beyond reach
Of name or word or Roman day.

Chapter VII: The Guardianship of the Land

The Gurt Wyrms retreated to the high heaths where the heather blooms like spilled wine across the hillside, and there they became the secret life within the whortleberries, their ancient bodies growing indistinguishable from the moorland itself.

They became protectors of the Exmoor ponies, breathing warmth into the winter air and guiding lost foals through the mist by instinct rather than design. They withdrew from human sight entirely, becoming what the human folk began to call The Great Log, or The Mossy Ridge, mistaken for landscape by those who had learned to see only with Roman eyes.

They guarded the untamed commons, those places where Roman law and human utility still feared to tread. Where the Gurt Wyrms slept, the land remembered its old ways. Straight paths became crooked again over time, boundaries blurred, the neat categories of Roman agriculture failed. Crops grew in strange spirals. Livestock wandered home by routes that appeared on no map. The Gurt Wyrms understood deep time in the way that empires never could: they knew that empires were brief fevers that passed and that the land would outlast every road ever driven through it.

To those few who still had ears to hear, the outcasts and wanderers and those who themselves refused categorisation, the Gurt Wyrms still sang their ancient law. They taught the old teaching: to protect is not to possess, to love is not to fix, to name is not always to know. This was a teaching that the Jinglewyrms had heard and eventually forgotten. It was a teaching that the Winderwyrms carried westward and across the entropic border into the Land of Farfrey, where it arrived, as all true teachings do, in the form of something practical and warm and edible.

I Am Not This, I am Not That

They became the hill itself in years,
The whortleberry, root and ridge,
Beyond the reach of Roman fears,
Beyond the mile-marked, measured bridge.

The ponies found their way by warmth
The Gurt Wyrm breathed in winter dark,
The foal through blinding mist led forth
By nothing visible: a spark.

To protect is not to possess,
To love is not to hold or fix,
To name is not to know the flesh
Of life that lives between the sticks.

They sang this law to those who heard,
The wanderers outside the frame,
The ones who could not be the word
That any ledger-keeper came

To write them down as. These few souls
Still heard the Gurt Wyrm in the mist
And learnt the law of patient wholes
And what the land does not resist.

Chapter VIII: The Woodcutter's Error

Centuries later, long after Rome had faded into half-remembered stone and the Latin tongue had softened into something else entirely, a woodcutter entered Shervage Wood. He was the heir, though he did not know it, to the Roman mindset of utility. He had never heard Latin spoken, had no love of empire, was in most respects an ordinary man with an ordinary axe and an ordinary need for timber. But he had been taught, as all those around him had been taught across a thousand years of Roman residue, to see the world as a resource, as timber and fuel, as things-for-humans.

He came upon a sleeping Gurt Wyrm, ancient beyond any measure a human being possesses, a being of profound and patient consciousness that had been dreaming slow dreams of geology since before the woodcutter's great-grandfather's great-grandfather drew his first breath. The woodcutter looked at it and saw only a massive oak, fallen and ripe for harvest. He ran his hand along the bark-scale and calculated board feet. He planned furniture, fence posts, firewood. He sharpened his axe on his whetstone, the scraping sound a violation of the deep silence of the wood. The Gurt Wyrm, dreaming of sandstone and slow time, did not wake.

The axe-blow was the Final Rupture, the violent act of a world that insists everything must be a thing to be cut and measured and sold. The blade bit deep. The Gurt Wyrm woke in agony, its scream not a sound but an earthquake, felt in every root from the Quantock Hills to Exmoor. As something between blood and sap and memory welled from the wound, the woodcutter finally saw what he had done. The oak was breathing. The moss was moving. The eyes that opened were older than his language. But understanding came too late to prevent, and could now only compound, the tragedy.

The Woodcutter And His Worry

He saw good timber in the grain,
He saw board feet and winter's need,
He raised the axe, no hate, no pain,
Just ordinary human greed.

The whetstone scraped. The silence broke.
The Gurt Wyrm dreamed of older stone.
He measured what appeared as oak
And raised the blade. He was alone.

No Roman told him what to see.
No edict shaped the axe's fall.
A thousand years of legacy
Had done that work, and done it all.

The blade bit deep. The wood breathed out.
The moss moved. Eyes of ancient years

Opened too late to speak or shout
Before the understanding clears.

Too late the knowing. Too late the care.
The slow disaster has no name
Quite like the ordinary there:
The well-intentioned, careful, same.

Chapter IX: The Sundering

The Gurt Wyrm was severed into two bleeding halves and this was the Forced Binary, the wholeness of the creature and the sacred ambiguity of its nature split by the blade of utility. What had been one became two. What had been both became neither. The wound was not merely physical but ontological, a rupture in the very possibility of existing outside of categories. In agony and confusion the two halves crawled in opposite directions, driven by an instinct older than thought: to survive, to escape, to find somewhere that the world still made sense.

But each was incomplete and each half remembered wholeness without being able to achieve it alone. One half recoiled toward Bilbrook, dragging itself through leaf mould, leaving a furrow that would become a stream. The other moved toward Kingston St Mary, crushing ferns beneath its weight, seeking a shelter it would never find. The ancient unity was lost. The land became a place of halves searching for the whole they could no longer remember.

Each half found a hollow and curled within it. Over days, then weeks, then months, they became stone, then fossil, then finally stratum, just another layer in the red sandstone that Caelir had once made bright with the gift of his own colour. The land accepted them back, but they were not at peace. The geology itself now bore the scar of their sundering. On certain nights, when the mist lies thick and the boundary between then and now grows thin, people in Bilbrook and Kingston St Mary report the same dream: of searching for something essential that was lost, of being incomplete, of reaching across an unbridgeable distance for a reunion that will never come.

An ancient Stone-Rhyme

What wholeness held in single form
Was halved by blade of utility,
The sacred middle, neither-nor,
Became a forced binary.

One half crawled west through Bilbrook's leaves,
And left a furrow, made a stream,
One east through Kingston's ferns and grieves,
In search of an impossible dream.

They curled in hollows. Became stone.
Became a fossil. Became red
Sandstone, and stratum, lying alone,
And were not at peace though the land said

Come home. Come home. The land said this.
But peace is not the same as rest.

The geology now holds the hiss
Of something halved within its breast.

And still on certain misty nights
Bilbrook and Kingston share one dream:
Of reaching across unbridged heights
To touch the half they cannot seem

To find again. The wound stays whole
In being unhealed. The scar in stone
Remembers still the single soul
That woke in pain, and died alone.

Chapter X: What Remains

What remains of the wyrm-kindreds is not what most would call a legacy. There are no great monuments, no carved stones bearing their names in any alphabet the Romans left behind. The Jinglewyrms are buried in red silt beneath the bay at Kilve, their copper scales long since oxidised past recognition. The sundered Gurt Wyrm of Shervage Wood is stratum in the sandstone, a geological fact that nobody alive can interpret. And yet.

The Gurt Wyrms remain in Shervage Wood, as they have always remained, in the deep sleep between one kind of world and the next. The bracken still stirs at the first rain of Spring. The ancient holly still creaks in the wind with a sound that is almost, but not quite, a voice. The Exmoor ponies still find their way home through the deepest fogs by routes that appear on no map made by human hands. These are not stories told to comfort anyone. They are simply what is still there, waiting with the particular patience of things that understand deep time.

The Winderwyrms, for their part, did not stay in Farfrey. They never do. Their entropic superposition, that living between the Physical and Unphysical Hollow Vale, means they are always in transit between what the world is and what it might become. They returned to Somerset with the Omega muffin's lesson written into their carmine bones, the understanding that the aggregate of all goodness is always accumulating, slowly, at half the speed of the easy choice but with twice the endurance. They are not a teaching. They are a practice.

Within the Land of Farfrey, the Winderwyrms bake even yet. The Snarleygogs, their seventeen chins somewhat thinned by the wearying of the years, have at last mastered the art of folding eggs with a delicate hand. The Zibbles observe all with their accustomed wisdom, while the Ploops keep their silent vigil from the corner. The eldest Zibble speaketh still of the V and its manifold branches, of the Omega and its slow accumulation, and of that K-value which measures the moral weight of an honest observation. The corner of Brimble and Squee grows warm as evening falls; and the muffins, as they are drawn from the oven, yield a scent for which no tongue hath a name. Yet every creature, in every province, between every Hollow Vale and beneath every distant orange sky, recognises it at once as the right thing done slowly, and the good thing done well.

In the old days, they piped tunes of a simple and jovial sort. Though such airs have largely vanished from the world's hearing, they linger yet in the stray melodies we whistle at our idle toil. Little do we know that these half-remembered echoes once possessed the power to make the very earth tremble, or caused the Winderwyrms to turn their great carmine heads toward the sound, recognising in our breath a thing they had long thought vanished. Perhaps they listen still. Perhaps the whistling is enough.

In Shervage Wood, where the bluebells bloom in Spring-time without the seeking of permission, and the paths refuse to keep a straight course, a certain spirit persists. It is not the Gurt Wyrms themselves—not in their fullness—but rather the principle they once embodied: that to be alive is to be in constant flux. Wholeness, after all, need not require a single shape. There be ways of existing that the Empire, in all its imperial might, never possessed the wit to imagine.

A child, being yet too young to have been shackled by the categories of men, sits amongst the timber on a Spring afternoon. She beholds a log that might be a wyrm, might be a dream, or might be the very land itself drawing breath. She reaches out a hand to find its surface and catches the scent of wild garlic, sharp and sudden, rising from nowhere. And for a moment, in that small, sun-warmed instant before the world hastens to explain itself, the wound begins to heal.

A Song For Somerset

The Gurt Wyrm sleeps in Shervage still,
The sandstone holds what it will keep,
No name upon no Roman sill,
Only the patient, carmine sleep.

The Winderwyrm does not remain
In any one place long enough
To leave a name. It comes again
Each Spring, in bracken, in the rough

Creak of the holly in the wind,
The thing that passes but is not
A thing you see. Something has thinned
The air and left it slightly hot.

The slow thing outlasts every road.
The patient thing outlasts the name.
The covenant, the ancient code,
Returns and always says the same:

To take what's needed, nothing more,
To give what's good and leave the rest,
To love the land you wandered for
And hold the waveform in your breast

Until the Omega is near,
Until the muffin rises true,
Until the slow thing makes it clear
That all of this was always you.

So whistle when you work the land,
Not knowing what the tune has kept,
The memory of an older hand
That held the world while empires slept.

A Curious Story of Britannia: Further History

Notes to Chapter I: The Hills Before Rome

The Quantock Hills are an Area of Outstanding Natural Beauty and the first designated AONB in England, so recognised in 1956, though the designation did nothing to improve the weather. The name Quantock derives from the Brittonic word Cantuc, meaning something close to the rim of a circle, which describes their shape with a geographical accuracy the Romans would have appreciated and the Winderwyrms would have found irrelevant. The hills are formed predominantly of Devonian sandstone, reddish in hue, and it is this particular redness that gave the local legend its most convenient detail.

The Gurt Worm of Shervage Wood is genuine Somerset folklore, not an invention of this book. Accounts of it circulated for centuries before being collected by folklorists in the nineteenth and early twentieth centuries, by which point the story had settled into a form in which a local man, discovering what he took to be a fallen log in Shervage Wood, was tricked into being eaten by the worm before another man cut the creature in two with a billhook. The two halves crawled apart, one toward Bilbrook and one toward Kingston St Mary, which accounts for a pleasing degree of geographical precision in a story that is otherwise not especially interested in accuracy. The folklorist Ruth Tongue collected and recorded this legend, and it is to her that most modern retellings owe their details, whether they acknowledge it or not.

Wild garlic, Allium ursinum, grows in considerable abundance in the damp woodland floors of Somerset in spring, and any walker through Shervage Wood or the Pardlestone valley in April will encounter it before they encounter anything else. Its smell is exactly as described: sharp, green, immediate, and impossible to confuse with anything else. That the barge-men of the old Bristol Channel coast developed a practical lore around it is invention on the part of this book, but an invention that feels earned.

Notes to Chapter II: The Jinglewyrms of Snarwood Bay

The beaches at Kilve in Somerset are among the richest fossil sites in England, composed of Lower Jurassic Liassic limestone and shale that erodes continuously into the foreshore. Ichthyosaur remains, ammonites, and other marine fossils are found there with regularity, and the beach has been a site of amateur and professional fossil hunting since the eighteenth century. That the Jinglewyrms might have emerged from these beds is not, given what the beds contain, entirely implausible.

The Roman lead and silver mining operations in the Mendip Hills were among the most economically significant in all of Roman Britain. Charterhouse-on-Mendip was the principal mining settlement, and lead pigs stamped with imperial marks and the abbreviation BRITT EX ARG have been recovered from the site, indicating that the mines were under direct imperial control from a very early point in the occupation. One such pig, dated to around 49 AD, barely six years after the Claudian invasion, suggests that the Romans moved to exploit the Mendip ore with a speed that would have impressed even the most efficiency-minded Jinglewyrm. The connection between the disturbance of underground silver seams and the restlessness of silver-scaled shore creatures is, admittedly, not attested in any Roman geological survey.

The Bristol Channel coastline in the Roman period supported considerable maritime trade, and Roman merchant vessels did anchor in the Somerset bays. Amphorae fragments have been recovered from coastal sites along the north Somerset coast, confirming the movement of goods including wine, olive oil and fish sauce into the region. Whether the Jinglewyrms surfaced at night to admire the coils of rope and the neat stacking of ceramic vessels is a matter on which the archaeological record is silent, though not, one feels, dismissively so.

Notes to Chapter III: The Winderwyrms of Farfrey

The Fosse Way is one of the great Roman roads of Britain, running from Exeter in the south-west to Lincoln in the north-east in a line so straight that it still impresses anyone who looks at it on a map. Through Somerset it runs north-east from Ilchester, passing through territory that the local Durotriges tribe had occupied for centuries before the Romans arrived and would continue to occupy, in various states of acquiescence and resentment, for centuries after. The road is still substantially intact in places and still serves as a road in others. It is, by any measure, a considerable piece of engineering, and the Winderwyrms' irritation at its failure to curve is entirely understandable.

The idea of ley lines, straight alignments connecting ancient sites across the landscape, was proposed by the amateur archaeologist Alfred Watkins in his 1921 book The Old Straight Track and has generated more argument per kilometre than almost any other idea in British folklore studies. Modern archaeology treats the concept with considerable scepticism, since the density of ancient sites in Britain is such that straight lines between them can be produced almost at will. The Winderwyrms, who navigate by older and more curved principles, would have no difficulty in distinguishing a true path from a surveyor's convenience.

The concept of entropic superposition as used in this book is not a technical term drawn from quantum mechanics, and no physicist should feel professionally implicated by its use here. It is borrowed and stretched in directions that its originators did not intend. The genuine quantum concept of superposition, in which a particle exists in multiple states simultaneously until observed, was formalised in the development of quantum mechanics in the 1920s and 1930s, principally through the work of Niels Bohr, Werner Heisenberg, and Erwin Schrodinger, whose unfortunate cat has become, through no fault of its own, one of the most over-referenced thought experiments in popular science writing. This book adds one more reference to that long list and does not apologise for it.

Notes to Chapter IV: Rome at the Shore

Aquae Sulis, the Roman settlement at Bath, was one of the most important religious and administrative sites in Roman Britain. The natural hot springs there, the only thermal springs in Britain, were sacred to the goddess Sulis before the Romans arrived and were dedicated to the composite deity Sulis Minerva during the Roman occupation. The great bathing complex was built over the course of the first and second centuries AD and remained in use until the Roman withdrawal. It is a measure of what the Romans left behind that the city of Bath has spent the subsequent sixteen centuries wondering what to do with the architecture.

The Second Legion Augusta, Legio II Augusta, was indeed the legion that accompanied Aulus Plautius in the Claudian invasion of 43 AD and was subsequently commanded by the future emperor Vespasian in campaigns across the south-west. Vespasian is recorded by the historian Suetonius as having fought thirty battles, subdued two fierce tribes, and captured more than twenty settlements during his western campaign, which included the reduction of the great Iron Age hillfort at Maiden Castle in Dorset. He later became Emperor in 69 AD after the Year of the Four Emperors, which is the kind of biographical detail that lends a certain weight to his presence in any history of Roman Somerset. The Capricorn was indeed the emblem of the Second Legion.

The practice of Roman timber surveying and resource assessment is well attested. Roman land surveyors, known as agrimensores, were trained professionals who used instruments including the groma and the chorobates to measure and record land, forests, water courses and mineral deposits with considerable precision. Their surveys formed the basis of Roman taxation and supply chain management, and fragments of their work survive in the Corpus Agrimensorum Romanorum, a collection of surveying texts copied in the medieval period. Whether any agrimensor named Decimus surveyed Shervage Wood is not recorded. The possibility cannot be ruled out.

Notes to Chapter V: The Charge of Betrayal

The Roman practice of granting titles and citizenship to compliant local leaders and communities was a central instrument of imperial administration throughout the empire, and Britain was no exception. Local aristocrats who demonstrated loyalty to Rome were incorporated into the Roman system through titles, trading privileges, and occasionally full citizenship. The result was a class of Romanised Britons who operated in the cultural borderland between their indigenous heritage and their adopted imperial identity, wearing both with varying degrees of comfort. The Jinglewyrms' Custodes Litoris designation is invented, but the social dynamic it represents was entirely real.

The destruction of indigenous libraries and repositories of knowledge during the Roman conquest of Britain is not well documented as a systematic policy, but the suppression of the Druids, who were the primary keepers of oral and written knowledge in pre-Roman Britain, was both deliberate and sustained. The Roman historian Tacitus records the destruction of the Druidic stronghold on the island of Mona, now Anglesey, in 60 AD, including the burning of sacred groves. Whether the Daughters of Avalon maintained a library at the White Spring of Glastonbury Tor and whether it was destroyed in this period are questions to which history gives no clear answer, which is precisely the kind of ambiguity that allows fiction to operate.

The transformation narrative of Myrdda into Myrddin draws on the long and complex history of the Merlin legend in British literature, which itself draws on the Welsh figure of Myrddin Wyllt, a prophetic wild man of the woods whose earliest textual appearances predate Geoffrey of Monmouth's Historia Regum Britanniae of around 1136. Geoffrey's Merlin is an amalgamation of several earlier figures and traditions. The name Myrddin is associated with Carmarthen, from the Brittonic Moridunum, and the figure appears in early Welsh poetry as both prophet and wild man. His origins in a female or non-binary figure are not part of the historical record but are not, given the flexibility of the tradition, an unreasonable extension of it.

Notes to Chapter VI: The Slaying of the Jinglewyrms

The Kilve beach coastline, where the Jinglewyrms are buried in the narrative, is genuinely rich in what might be mistaken for wyrm remains. The Liassic blue lias limestone that forms the foreshore weathers into long, curved sections that lie across the rock platform in formations that have prompted imaginative interpretation for as long as people have walked there. Ichthyosaur skeletons have been recovered from the cliffs above the beach, and it is not difficult to see how a coastal people might have read these curved, ribbed remains as the bones of something that had once lived rather than something that had drowned in the Jurassic sea two hundred million years before. Folklore is often the longest-surviving form of geological record.

The three days of mourning described at the end of the chapter, in which no bird sang on the Somerset coast, draws on a widespread motif in British and Irish folklore in which the land itself responds to great events through the behaviour of birds and animals. It is attested in numerous sources from the medieval period onward and reflects a cosmological understanding of the natural world as responsive and communicative that was common to most pre-modern cultures in Britain. The ornithologist would note that complete silence among coastal birds is functionally impossible under normal circumstances. The folklorist would note that folklore is not obligated to check with the ornithologist.

The oxidisation of copper and silver in saltwater environments is a genuine chemical process, and copper objects recovered from coastal and marine archaeological sites in Britain do present in the dull, greenish state described. Roman copper alloy objects recovered from the Somerset Levels and coastal sites are often in poor condition as a result of long immersion in the particular mineral cocktail of west country coastal sediment. That the Jinglewyrms' scales underwent the same transformation is a piece of scientific plausibility that arrived in the narrative by accident and was retained on its merits.

Notes to Chapter VII: The Guardianship of the Land

The Exmoor pony is one of the oldest native breeds in Britain, with a history on the moor that is believed by some researchers to extend back to the late Pleistocene, making it a plausible companion for creatures of the wyrm's antiquity. The breed is characterised by its hardiness, its ability to navigate moorland terrain in poor visibility, and its broad mealy nose, which is a practical adaptation to the Exmoor climate and not, so far as is known, an indication of any guidance from sleeping Gurt Wyrms. The Exmoor Pony Society was founded in 1921 and the breed is now classified as endangered, with fewer than five hundred breeding mares in existence.

The concept of the commons, land held in common use by the community rather than in private ownership, was central to the agricultural and social organisation of medieval Somerset and of most of rural Britain before the enclosures of the eighteenth and nineteenth centuries. Exmoor itself retains significant areas of common land, and the Quantock Hills include commons at Holford and elsewhere. These were and remain places where the usual rules of private ownership and utility do not fully apply, which lends them a quality that the Gurt Wyrms would recognise. The enclosure movement, which replaced common land with private fields across much of England between roughly 1750 and 1850, can be understood as the woodcutter's error at a national scale.

The pattern of straight Roman roads reverting to curved and wandering routes over time is observable across Britain wherever Roman road alignments have been superseded by medieval and later tracks. Medieval people navigated by landmarks, hills, boundaries and water courses rather than by geometric survey, and the roads they created reflect this. The Fosse Way is a partial exception, having remained substantially in use for most of its length, but even its course has been diverted and curved by the needs of subsequent settlements in ways that would have distressed its original surveyors considerably.

Notes to Chapter VIII: The Woodcutter's Error

Shervage Wood is a real wood on the eastern edge of the Quantock Hills, now managed by the Forestry Commission, containing a mixture of oak, conifer plantation, and areas of more ancient woodland structure. It is the specific wood named in the Gurt Worm legend as the creature's home, and the killing of the worm by a woodcutter who mistook it for a fallen log is the central event of that legend as collected by Ruth Tongue. The detail that the woodcutter was carrying cider and sat down to eat his lunch on what he took to be a convenient log, only to discover his error when the log began to move, is one of the more vivid pieces of Somerset folklore in the record.

Medieval woodcutting in England was a highly regulated activity, governed by systems of coppicing, pollarding and managed felling that were designed to sustain woodland productivity across decades and centuries. The woodcutter of the chapter, working alone with an axe and a whetstone, represents a later, less regulated tradition, possibly post-medieval, in which woodland was managed as a private resource rather than a common one. The distinction matters because the regulated woodland worker of the medieval period had, by necessity, a more intimate understanding of the wood as a living system than the man who arrived to cut and take. The chapter's woodcutter is not malicious. He is simply the product of a tradition that had, by his time, forgotten what it once knew.

The geological slow time invoked in the chapter is not merely a literary device. The red sandstone of the Quantock Hills is Devonian in origin, formed approximately 380 to 360 million years ago from sediments deposited in a semi-arid environment quite unlike the wet Somerset landscape it now underlies. To dream of sandstone is, if you think about it, to dream of a time before the British Isles existed in any form a human would recognise, before the Atlantic Ocean opened, before the chalk of southern England was laid down in warm Cretaceous seas. The Gurt Wyrm's geology dreams are, if anything, understated.

Notes to Chapter IX: The Sundering

Bilbrook is a real hamlet in Somerset, lying west of Shervage Wood near the village of Washford on the edge of Exmoor, and Kingston St Mary is a real village to the east, near Taunton. These are the two locations named in collected versions of the Gurt Worm legend as the destinations of the two severed halves, and their appearance here is not invention but fidelity to the source. The geographical distance between them is approximately fourteen kilometres, which is either a measure of the Gurt Wyrm's original size or of the distance over which a severed creature might be expected to crawl before giving up. The stream at Bilbrook is real and runs, as described, through leaf mould and soft ground toward the sea.

The geological concept of a fossil becoming stratum is accurate. Fossilisation is a process by which organic material is replaced over millions of years by mineral compounds, and the resulting fossil becomes, in time, indistinguishable from the rock matrix that surrounds it. In the red sandstone and blue lias of Somerset, fossils are abundant and often identifiable only by careful examination of the rock surface. The geologist's field hammer and the folklorist's notebook are, in Somerset, useful companions.

The shared dream as a folk motif, in which people separated by distance report experiencing the same dream, is widespread in British and Irish tradition and appears in a number of Somerset stories collected in the late nineteenth and early twentieth centuries. It is generally associated with places where something significant has occurred and is understood as a form of memory held not in individual minds but in the landscape itself. Whether the people of Bilbrook and Kingston St Mary report such dreams today is a question that would require a sociological survey this book is not equipped to conduct, though the author notes that nobody has definitively ruled it out.

Notes to Chapter X: What Remains

The bluebells of Shervage Wood are real and arrive in spring in the manner described, without asking permission and without particular respect for the paths that human walkers have made through the wood. British bluebells, Hyacinthoides non-scripta, are a specific indicator species of ancient woodland, meaning that their presence in a wood is generally taken as evidence that the woodland has existed continuously for at least four hundred years, and often considerably longer. A wood full of bluebells in spring is, in this sense, a wood that has been remembering itself for centuries before any map was made of it.

The Gurt Worm legend has survived into the twenty-first century through the work of collectors including Ruth Tongue, whose 1965 book Somerset Folklore remains a standard reference, and through the efforts of local historians and the Somerset Folklore Society. It is told to children in Somerset schools and appears on local signage in the Quantock Hills. The fact that it is known at all is itself a form of the principle the legend encodes: that the slow thing, the thing passed mouth to mouth across the generations without institutional support or commercial incentive, sometimes outlasts the fast thing carved in stone.

The child in the wood at the end of the chapter is not a real child known to the author. She is a composite of every child who has ever sat in a British woodland and felt, without being able to explain why, that the wood was thinking about something. This is not a mystical claim. It is a description of what attention feels like when it is given freely, without agenda, to a place that has been alive for longer than any category we have for it. The wild garlic smell that arrives from nowhere at the end of the chapter is real in the sense that wild garlic does arrive from nowhere, suddenly and completely, in Somerset woods in spring. What it means when it does is, as always in Somerset, left to the observer.

Bibliography and Further Reading

Bennett, G. and Smith, P. eds. (1996) *Contemporary Legend: A Reader. New York: Garland.*

Briggs, K.M. (1967) *The Fairies in English Tradition and Literature. London: Routledge and Kegan Paul.*

Briggs, K.M. (1970-71) *A Dictionary of British Folk-Tales in the English Language. 4 vols. London: Routledge.*

British Geological Survey (n.d.) *Online Geology Viewer. Available at: maps.bgs.ac.uk (Accessed: as required).*

Bromwich, R. (2006) *Trioedd Ynys Prydein: The Welsh Triads. 3rd edn. Cardiff: University of Wales Press.*

Campbell, B. (2000) *The Writings of the Roman Land Surveyors: Introduction, Text, Translation and Commentary. London: Society for the Promotion of Roman Studies.*

Clarke, B. trans. (1973) *Life of Merlin: Vita Merlini by Geoffrey of Monmouth. Cardiff: University of Wales Press.*

Craddock, P. (2009) *Scientific Investigation of Copies, Fakes and Forgeries.* Oxford: Butterworth-Heinemann.

Cunliffe, B. (1985) and Davenport, P. *The Temple of Sulis Minerva at Bath.* 2 vols. Oxford: Oxford University Committee for Archaeology.

Cunliffe, B. (2000) *Roman Bath Discovered.* 4th edn. Stroud: Tempus.

Cunliffe, B. (2001) *Facing the Ocean: The Atlantic and its Peoples, 8000 BC to AD 1500.* Oxford: Oxford University Press.

Cunliffe, B. (2010) *Druids: A Very Short Introduction.* Oxford: Oxford University Press.

Devereux, P. (2003) *Fairy Paths and Spirit Roads.* London: Vega.

Ekwall, E. (1960) *The Concise Oxford Dictionary of English Place-Names.* 4th edn. Oxford: Oxford University Press.

Exmoor Pony Society (n.d.) *Breed History and Conservation.* Available at: exmoorponysociety.org.uk (Accessed: as required).

Frere, S. (1987) *Britannia: A History of Roman Britain.* 3rd edn. London: Routledge.

Geoffrey of Monmouth (c.1136) *Historia Regum Britanniae.* Translated by L. Thorpe (1966) *The History of the Kings of Britain.* London: Penguin Classics.

Green, M. (1997) *The World of the Druids.* London: Thames and Hudson.

Greenwood, B. (1996) *The Exmoor Pony.* Tiverton: Exmoor Books.

Gribbin, J. (1984) *In Search of Schrodinger's Cat: Quantum Physics and Reality.* London: Bantam.

House, M. (1993) *Geology of the Dorset Coast.* London: Geologists' Association.

International Commission on Stratigraphy (n.d.) *International Chronostratigraphic Chart.* Available at: stratigraphy.org (Accessed: as required).

Jackson, J. trans. (1931-37) *Annals by Tacitus.* 4 vols. Loeb Classical Library. Cambridge, MA: Harvard University Press.

Jarman, A.O.H. (1960) *The Legend of Merlin.* Cardiff: University of Wales Press.

Mann, J.C. and Penman, R.G. eds. (1978) *Literary Sources for Roman Britain.* Lactor 11. London: London Association of Classical Teachers.

Margary, I.D. (1973) *Roman Roads in Britain.* 3rd edn. London: John Baker.

Millett, M. (1990) *The Romanization of Britain: An Essay in Archaeological Interpretation.* Cambridge: Cambridge University Press.

Mills, A.D. (2003) *A Dictionary of British Place-Names.* Oxford: Oxford University Press.

Natural England (n.d.) *Quantock Hills AONB Management Plan.* Available at: naturalengland.org.uk (Accessed: as required).

Neeson, J.M. (1993) *Commoners: Common Right, Enclosure and Social Change in England, 1700-1820.* Cambridge: Cambridge University Press.

O'Sullivan, S. (1942) *A Handbook of Irish Folklore*. Dublin: Folklore of Ireland Society. Reprinted (1970) Detroit: Singing Tree Press.

Peterken, G. (1981) *Woodland Conservation and Management*. London: Chapman and Hall.

Plantlife (n.d.) *Ancient Woodland Indicator Species*. Available at: plantlife.org.uk (Accessed: as required).

Prothero, D. (2013) *Bringing Fossils to Life: An Introduction to Paleobiology*. 3rd edn. New York: Columbia University Press.

Rackham, O. (1980) *Ancient Woodland: Its History, Vegetation and Uses in England*. London: Edward Arnold.

Rackham, O. (1986) *The History of the Countryside*. London: Dent.

Rackham, O. (1990) *Trees and Woodland in the British Landscape*. Revised edn. London: Dent.

Rodwell, J.S. ed. (1991) *British Plant Communities*. Vol. 1. Cambridge: Cambridge University Press.

Rolfe, J.C. trans. (1914) *The Lives of the Caesars by Suetonius*. 2 vols. Loeb Classical Library. Cambridge, MA: Harvard University Press.

Roman Amphorae: a digital resource (n.d.) University of Southampton. Available at: ads.ahds.ac.uk (Accessed: as required).

Salway, P. (1981) *Roman Britain*. Oxford: Oxford University Press.

Sharples, N. (1991) *Maiden Castle: Excavations and Field Survey 1985-6*. London: English Heritage.

Simpson, J. (1980) *British Dragons*. London: Batsford.

Simpson, J. and Roud, S. (2000) *A Dictionary of English Folklore*. Oxford: Oxford University Press.

Tate, W.E. (1978) *A Domesday of English Enclosure Acts and Awards*. Reading: University of Reading.

Taylor, C. (1979) *Roads and Tracks of Britain*. London: Dent.

Tongue, R.L. (1965) *Somerset Folklore*. Ed. K.M. Briggs. London: Folklore Society.

Tylecote, R. (1992) *A History of Metallurgy*. 2nd edn. London: Maney Publishing.

Victoria County History of Somerset (various dates). Available at: british-history.ac.uk (Accessed: as required).

Watkins, A. (1925) *The Old Straight Track*. London: Methuen. Reprinted (1970) London: Garnstone Press.

Wheeler, J. and Zurek, W. eds. (1983) *Quantum Theory and Measurement*. Princeton: Princeton University Press.

Williamson, T. and Bellamy, L. (1983) *Ley Lines in Question*. Kingswood: World's Work.

Woodland Trust (n.d.) *Ancient Woodland and Bluebell Surveys*. Available at: woodlandtrust.org.uk (Accessed: as required).

Schrodinger, E. (1935) 'Die gegenwärtige Situation in der Quantenmechanik', *Naturwissenschaften*, 23, pp. 807-812, 823-828, 844-849.

Glossary: Places and History

Aquae Sulis: The Roman name for Bath, Somerset, meaning Waters of Sulis, after the goddess of the hot spring that the Romans co-opted and dedicated to their own Minerva, as was their habit with things they found and could not quite explain. The governors of Roman Britannia maintained administrative functions here well into the late period of occupation. The waters are still warm. The Romans are not.

Avalonae: The Tharionese name for Avalon, the great mythic isle of the western tradition, here rendered as a real place in the cosmology of the Hollow Vale rather than a purely legendary one. Its relationship to Glastonbury Tor is, as with most things in Somerset, complicated by fog.

Bilbrook: A hamlet on the western edge of the Quantock Hills near the village of Washford, lying in the direction of Exmoor. In Somerset folklore it is the destination of one half of the Gurt Worm after its sundering, the half that dragged itself westward through the leaf mould of Shervage Wood and left behind a furrow that became, in time, a stream. The hamlet exists. The stream exists. The rest is a matter of what you choose to believe about the sandstone.

Bodmin Moor: A high moorland plateau in Cornwall, bleak and wet and home to a significant number of things that the Ordnance Survey declines to map. The wise hog of this book makes her home here, which is consistent with the moor's general character as a place where ancient and knowing things have retreated from the world and are waiting, with some patience, to be found by the right kind of person.

Brimble Street and Squee: The corner in the Land of Farfrey from which the narrator observes the Great Bake-Off. It is not on any map of Somerset or anywhere else, and it is not intended to be. It is, however, warm in the evenings.

Bristol Channel: The wide tidal estuary separating Somerset and the rest of south Wales, down which the Roman trade galleys came and through which the barge-men of the old coast navigated with the particular confidence of people who have memorised every sandbank. The Jinglewyrms heard the merchant vessels before they saw them, on still nights when the bell-voices carried.

Buronium: The Tharionese name for Burnham-on-Sea, or possibly Bridgwater, or possibly a composite of several north Somerset coastal settlements. The precise identification is disputed among scholars of the Tharion Cycle, of whom there are, at present, very few.

Cadbury: South Cadbury in Somerset, site of a substantial Iron Age hillfort that has been associated with the Arthurian legend of Camelot since at least the sixteenth century when the antiquary John Leland visited and reported local tradition to that effect. Whether King Arthur held court here, whether

King Arthur existed at all, and whether any of this matters to the Snarleygogs are questions this book leaves open.

Cantoc Tor: The Tharionese name for the Quantock Hills, deriving from the Brittonic word *Cantuc* meaning the rim of a circle, which describes their shape with geographical accuracy. They are also known, in the modern period, as the Quantocks, and in this book as the hills that outlasted the Romans, which is the description that counts.

Charterhouse-on-Mendip: The principal Roman mining settlement in the Mendip Hills, where lead and silver were extracted under direct imperial control from the earliest decades of the occupation. Lead pigs stamped with imperial marks have been recovered from the site. Whether the Jinglewyrms were present at the first shaft-sinking is not attested in Roman records.

Exmoor: A high plateau of moorland on the Somerset and Devon border, home to the Exmoor pony, the red deer, the whortleberry, and, in this book, the sleeping Gurt Wyrms who retreated here after the slaying of the Jinglewyrms and became indistinguishable from the landscape. The National Park designation came in 1954 and did not disturb them.

Falmouth: A harbour town in Cornwall at the mouth of the Fal estuary, one of the deepest natural harbours in the world. In this book it is where Myrdda begins her journey, having watched a thorn tree die at the Mouth of Ffall in circumstances that are not the Romans' fault only in the sense that most things in Roman Britain were not the Romans' fault in that direct way.

Farfrey: A land that does not appear on any human map because it exists, as the Winderwyrms understand, only when observed. Its sky is orange. Its grass is blue. Its air is thick enough to chew like cheese. It sits in the space between the collapsing of one moral waveform and the rising of the next, which is why the Winderwyrms found it by accident and why they have never entirely found their way out of it. The location of the corner of Brimble and Squee within Farfrey is not specified.

Ffall, Mouth of: A coastal location in Cornwall or west Somerset, possibly slightly north of Falmouth, possibly a Tharionese rendering of a real place-name that has since changed beyond recognition. It is where Myrdda's thorn tree died and where her story, and Merlin's, begins.

Fowey: A harbour town in Cornwall on the estuary of the River Fowey, mentioned in this book as a staging point on Myrdda's journey from Falmouth northward toward Bodmin Moor and the Snarleygogs. The town is real and the estuary is beautiful and neither of them has any comment to make about the Snarleygogs.

Glastonbury Tor: A hill rising abruptly from the Somerset Levels near the town of Glastonbury, topped by the roofless tower of the medieval church of St Michael. In pre-Roman times, before the Levels were drained, the Tor stood as an island in a wide marsh. It is Tor Velden in the Tharionese of this book, and the White Spring at its foot, known as the Hwit Fford, is the location of the druidic ritual described in the Perdix chapter. The spring is real and still flows.

Grumblesome Hill: The name given in this book to the hill in the Land of Farfrey where the Snarleygogs make their home, from which they conduct their operations of resentment, muffin-baking, and competitive grumbling. It is not a real hill, but anyone who has spent time in Somerset will recognise its character.

Hinclaeth: The Tharionese name for Hinkley Point on the Somerset coast, where the Severn Estuary narrows and the tidal range becomes one of the highest in the world. The Barge House chapter is set here, in the year 100 AD, during a period of relative peace under the Emperor Trajan. The nuclear power station that now occupies the headland is not discussed in this book.

Hollow Vale, The Physical: The physical world as the Winderwyrms and Gurt Wyrms understand it: the earth, the stone, the bracken, the living things. Not, in their cosmology, the primary residence.

Hollow Vale, The Unphysical: The other state of being, neither dream nor death but something adjacent to both, in which the Winderwyrms spend considerable time and from which they access Farfrey and other lands unknown to human cartography. Entropic superposition between the two Vales is their natural condition and their persistent inconvenience.

Kelvenna: The Tharionese name for Kilve, a village and beach on the north Somerset coast between Bridgwater Bay and the Quantock Hills. The beach is formed of Liassic limestone and shale and is rich in fossil marine reptiles. The Jinglewyrms rose here, in this book, from the fossil beds. In the present day, amateur fossil hunters find ichthyosaur remains in the cliff exposures above the foreshore and do not always look closely enough at what else the rock might contain.

Kilve: See *Kelvenna*. The modern name. The beach is free to visit. The fossils belong to the landowner unless the foreshore is below mean high water, in which case they belong to the Crown, which is a distinction the Jinglewyrms would have understood perfectly.

Kingston St Mary: A village to the east of the Quantock Hills, near Taunton, named in Somerset folklore as the destination of the second half of the sundered Gurt Worm. It lies approximately fourteen kilometres from Bilbrook in a straight line across the hills. In this book, the people of Kingston St Mary and Bilbrook share a dream, on certain misty nights, of something reaching for something else across an unbridgeable distance. The village is real. The dream is reported.

Lugdunum: The Roman name for Lyon in modern France, here mentioned as the retirement destination of the young surveyor from Gaul who saw the moss move in Shervage Wood and never ate wild garlic again. Whether he returned to Lyon or remained in Britain is not recorded. He is not a real person.

Mendip Hills: A range of limestone hills in Somerset running east to west to the south of the Quantock country, beneath which the Romans found lead and silver ore in quantities that drove their extraction operations for the duration of the occupation. The hills are now known for their caves, their cider orchards, and the Cathedral city of Wells at their southern edge. The mines at Charterhouse are largely grassed over.

Mona: The Roman name for the island of Anglesey in north Wales, where the Druidic stronghold was destroyed by Roman forces in 60 AD in an operation recorded by Tacitus, including the burning of the sacred groves. This is the event from which the burning of the Daughters of Avalon's library at Glastonbury is extrapolated in this book, at considerable geographical and chronological distance.

Pardlestone: A hamlet in the Quantock Hills, set in a wooded combe on the western slopes of the hills near the village of

Holford. The woodlands here are ancient, damp, and, in spring, carpeted in wild garlic and bluebells in the sequence described in Chapter I. The Gurt Wyrms descended here on rainy days.

Paritonum: The Tharionese name for Bridgwater, or possibly Parrett-mouth, the settlement at the mouth of the River Parrett on Bridgwater Bay. In the Caradoc and Brannoc chapter of the original Hollow Vale book, it is named as one of the three ports of the ancient Trinity of coastal trade, the one that broke faith with the Romans during the invasion and whose treachery silenced the Whisperflow and turned the wells of Buronium to brine.

Quantock Hills: The range of Devonian sandstone hills in Somerset running northwest to southeast between Bridgwater Bay and Taunton, designated in 1956 as England's first Area of Outstanding Natural Beauty. The name derives from the Brittonic *Cantuc*, meaning the rim or circle. They are red-soiled and heathered at the top, wooded on the combes, and have been home to the Gurt Wyrms since before the Romans came and will be home to them after everyone else has finished discussing it.

Saelhara: The Tharionese or fictional name for the Sahara Desert, the setting for the earliest section of *The Sundered Land* preview, in which Mira and the Arthons begin their journey northward toward the island that will become Britain. It is approximately 2500 BC. The rains have come. Everything that follows takes a long time.

Shervage Wood: A wood on the eastern edge of the Quantock Hills, now managed by the Forestry Commission, containing ancient oak and more recent conifer planting. It is the specific wood named in the Gurt Worm legend of Somerset as the creature's home, and the location of the woodcutter's error. If you visit in spring, the wild garlic is abundant. If you see a very large fallen log, the barge-men's wisdom applies.

Snarwood Bay: The bay on the north Somerset coast in which the Jinglewyrms made their home, described in this book as part of the Kilve and Snarwood Bay shoreline. Snarwood is a name that does not appear on modern Ordnance Survey maps and may be a Tharionese rendering of a local or historical name for a section of that coast, or may be invented, or both.

Somerset: The county. Known as Tharion in the cosmology of this book, deriving from an older name that the Roman occupation slowly displaced. A fogged region of hearty folk, wild wyrms, deep magick, excessive rainfall, excellent cider, and a tradition of quietly remembering things that the rest of England has chosen to forget.

Tharion: The Tharionese name for Somerset, used throughout the Tharion Cycle of which this book is a part. Its etymology within the fiction relates to the ancient covenants of Caelir The One and the original naming of the land before Roman occupation. Its relationship to the real historical place-names of the region, including Somersetae (from which Somerset derives), is suggestive rather than literal.

Tor Velden: The Tharionese name for Glastonbury Tor. See *Glastonbury Tor*.

Wumble, The (Trees and Stable of): Wumble trees grow in the Land of Farfrey in shades that have no name in Somerset. Old Wumble's Stable, near which the Great Farfrey Bake-Off table was set up, is a landmark in Farfrey of sufficient age and reputation that no Zibble, Plonk, Wibble, Ploop or Snorf has ever thought to question its presence there. The tree's relationship to the Wumble-tree mayors, who lack authority over the Winderwyrms, is unclear. It is possible there is only one Wumble.

Whisperflow, The: A sacred watercourse in the Tharionese cosmology, running through or near Glastonbury, which in the Caradoc and Brannoc chapter is described as having fallen silent as a consequence of the treachery of the merchants of Paritonum. It carried currents of the Wyrd to the great Bell of Avalonae, and its silence was a calamity. Whether it still flows, silently or otherwise, beneath the present drainage ditches of the Somerset Levels is a question the hydrological survey has not addressed.

The Compendium of the Vales: A Combined Appendix

Appendix A: The Roman Occupation and the Leaden Silence

The arrival of Legio II Augusta in 43 AD brought a rigid, geometric reality to the Southwest. The Romans were primarily interested in the silver and lead deposits at Charterhouse-on-Mendip, and they extracted both with an efficiency that the Mendip Hills have not entirely forgiven. To the Gurt Wyrms, the mines were deep, weeping sores in the sandstone that Caelir The One had coloured red for reasons the Romans never thought to ask about.

The Jinglewyrms appeared during this era, seemingly born from the silver-bleed of the disturbed earth. Some of the older barge-men believed they were not merely attracted to Roman silver but were in some sense made of it: spirits of the ore-seams given wing and voice by the disturbance of mining. The construction of the Fosse Way acted as what the

Winderwyrms, in their more candid moments, called a moral blade. In Somerset folklore it is whispered that the road's near-straight line cut through the winding Ley-paths of the Wyrms, forcing many into the Unphysical Hollow Vale as they could no longer traverse a land so strictly partitioned. The Fosse Way is still there. The Ley-paths are harder to find but have not gone anywhere.

The Second Legion, Legio II Augusta, was commanded in the western campaigns by the future emperor Vespasian, who subdued the Durotriges tribe and reduced the great hillfort at Maiden Castle. He later became Emperor in 69 AD, which is the kind of biographical arc that lends a certain weight to his presence in any history of Roman Somerset. The Capricorn was the emblem of the Second Legion. The Quantock Hills did not find this impressive.

Appendix B: The Straight-Blade Report

Fragment of a letter from Decurion Marcus Flavianus, c. 62 AD, discovered in a lead-lined casket in 1904.

"The surveyors are in a state of near-mutiny. We have attempted to lay the road-line according to the Governor's decree, but the Quantock sandstone seems to shift beneath the chains. The men complain of a scent, a heavy, choking cloud of wild garlic, that arises even where no plants grow. More troubling are the Jinglers at the coast. My men have lost three weeks' pay to the air itself; they claim the copper coins simply jingled away toward the tide-line. The hills do not want our straight lines; they prefer to wind, and in their winding, we lose our sense of Rome."

Field Survey Log, Cantoc District, Day 14. Chain measurement inconclusive for the third consecutive morning. Lead weights register correctly at base camp but deviate by approximately two Roman feet when deployed above the sandstone ridge. Surveyor's assistant Caius reports hearing what he describes as singing from the rock face. I have recorded this as wind. The road-line will require revision. Again.

Wax tablet fragment, Mendip mining district, date unknown. Badly damaged. Final sentence only legible: "And the silver was not where the surveys said it would be, but the holes we dug were already there."

Latin Version:

"Mensores paene seditionem movent. Viam ex edicto Legati derigere conati sumus, sed saxa Cantocensia sub catenis mutari videntur. Milites de odore queruntur, gravi et strangulante alii silvestris nebula, quae exoritur ubi nulla planta crescit. Magis autem me movent Tinnuli illi maritimi. Homines mei stipendium trium septimanarum in ipsum aërem amiserunt; dicunt nummos aeneos ad aestum tinnientes abscessisse. Montes lineas nostras rectas non patiuntur; flecti malunt, et flexu eorum sensum Romae amittimus.

Field Survey Log, Cantoc District, Day 14: Dimensio catenarum tertio quoque mane irrita. Libramina in castris recte se habent, sed super iugum saxeum duos circiter pedes Romanos aberrant. Caius adiutor se cantum e rupe audire refert. Pro vento hoc annotavi. Linea viae iterum mutanda erit. Denuo.

Wax tablet fragment, Mendip mining district, date unknown: ...et argentum non illic erat ubi nuntiatum erat, sed foveas quas fodimus iam ibi invenimus."

Appendix C: Geographical Gazetteer of Somerset and Farfrey

Shervage Wood (pronounced Sher-vidge): The ancestral seat of the Gurt Wyrms. The Singularity of Shervage is the exact point where the Wyrm Spindle is loudest, and the specific location of the woodcutter's error. Managed today by the Forestry Commission. Wild garlic is abundant in spring. The large fallen log rule applies.

Kilve Beach (Tharionese: Kelvenna): The Oil-Beaches, rich in Liassic ammonite and ichthyosaur fossils. The Jinglewyrms emerge here from the red silt fossil beds. Fossils still surface regularly in the cliff exposures. The barge-men who once navigated Bridgwater Bay knew to listen for the bell-voices before they saw the shore.

Pardlestone Combe: One of the deep wooded valleys on the western side of the Quantock Hills, damp enough in March to feel submerged. Wild garlic fills it from late April. The Gurt Wyrms descended here on rainy days from the ridge above.

The Fosse Way (Tharionese: The Straight-Blade): Running northeast from Exeter to Lincoln, entering Somerset near Axminster. To the Gurt Wyrms it was not merely a road but an ontological statement: a declaration that the land's own curvature was an error requiring correction. The road remains. In places it is still straight. In places the land has quietly reasserted its preference for curves.

Glastonbury Tor (Tharionese: Tor Velden): A hill rising abruptly from the Somerset Levels, topped by the tower of the medieval church of St Michael. Before the Levels were drained it stood as an island in a wide marsh. The White Spring at its foot (Hwit Fford) is the location of the druidic ritual in the Perdix chapter. The spring still flows.

The Whisperflow: The sacred underground watercourse connecting the White Spring to the wider Wyrd-network of Tharion. Its silencing, following the treachery of the merchants of Paritonum, is described in the Caradoc and Brannoc chapter. Whether it still flows beneath the Victorian drainage channels of the Somerset Levels is a question the hydrological survey has not addressed.

The Mouth of Ffall: The coastal inlet in west Cornwall where Myrdda's thorn tree died and her transformation began. The name may derive from the Cornish *fal*, meaning a cliff or promontory. The thorn tree is gone. The wind off that coast is unchanged.

Bilbrook: A hamlet on the western edge of the Quantock Hills, near Washford. The destination of one half of the Gurt Wyrm after its sundering. The furrow it left became a stream. Both the hamlet and the stream exist.

Kingston St Mary: A village east of the Quantock Hills, near Taunton. The destination of the second half. Approximately fourteen kilometres from Bilbrook in a straight line across the hills. On certain misty nights, people in both places report the same dream.

Brimble-and-Squee Streets: A liminal crossroads in Farfrey where the Wumble trees grow thickest. Whistling a Somerset tune here causes the orange sky to turn the carmine colour of a Winderwyrm's wing.

Grumblesome Hill: The highest point of moral ugliness in Farfrey and the permanent residence of the Snarleygogs.

Old Wumble's Stable: Adjacent to the site of the Great Farfrey Bake-Off. Whether Old Wumble was a creature, a person, or a Wumble tree of unusual age, the text does not specify. The stable smells of something warm that is not quite hay.

Appendix D: Biology and Taxonomy of the Wyrm-Kinds

Biotic Mimicry and Taxonomy: The Wyrm-Kinds of Somerset and Farfrey

Biotic Mimicry: In Somerset natural history, the Wyrms exhibit Biotic Mimicry, a process by which they entrain with the local minerals over long periods of geological time. This is not merely camouflage but a fundamental shift in their physical composition to match the ancient architecture of the land.

Moss-Backs: As Gurt Wyrms age, their metabolic rate slows to a Quantum Crawl. Their skin takes on the properties of Devonian Red Sandstone, making them indistinguishable from rock until they breathe—a process occurring once every seven years. The woodcutter's hand on the bark-scale felt something older than timber and did not stop to consider what this meant. These Wyrms, found primarily in Shervage Wood and the deep earth, possess a stoic and patient temperament, characterized by a slow waveform collapse and a high Omega value.

The Lichen Bond: Winderwyrms maintain a symbiotic relationship with Usnea, also known as Old Man's Beard. These plants act as quantum antennae, allowing them to navigate the entropic superposition between the Physical and

Unphysical Vales. The Fosse Way disrupted this navigation system because straight lines produce no Usnea and offer no purchase for the Ley-paths. These restless, curious observers of the Hollow Vales and Farfrey possess shifting, translucent scales and exist in a state of constant entropic superposition.

The Silver Scales: Jinglewyrms possess scales of copper and silver mail that jingle like Roman denarii dropped into a hollow bowl. Unlike their cousins, they crave boundaries and surfaces that reflect light with certainty. The disturbance of the Mendip silver seams appears to have activated their emergence from the fossil beds at Kilve, suggesting a mineral sensitivity that predates their coastal habitat by some considerable geological time. These order-obsessed creatures of Snarwood Bay often experience a fast waveform collapse, leading to half-value outcomes.

Snarleygog Biology: The Snarleygogs of Grumblesome Hill possess seventeen chins apiece, more than any chin-based function requires. The surplus chins are given over entirely to grumbling, which proceeds in a remarkable range of tones. Their temperament is often described as hostile, which is not quite accurate; it is competitive.

The difference matters because it means the Snarleygog is always paying attention to the Winderwyrm's muffin, which is how the youngest one, with only nine chins, eventually asked the right question. Their state remains uncollapsed but is increasingly tending toward resolution.

Appendix E: Lexicon of the Hollow Vale

Ark at 'ee: Lit. "Listen to him/her." A command to pay attention to the spiritual K-value of a moment. From the

Somerset dialect Arketh'ee, still used in the west country in its colloquial form.

The Gable: Slang for Roman civilisation; the desire to put a roof or limit over the wild, entropic world. The pitched roof divides; the Hollow Vale does not.

Gurt: Westcountry dialect for Great. Implies ancient, tectonic mass rather than mere size. A gurt thing has been great for a long time.

The Hollow Vale: The space between the Physical and Unphysical states of being. Neither world nor dream. The natural residence of the Winderwyrms and the destination of anything that refuses to be categorised.

K-value: The efficiency score of moral observation. The higher the K-value of those watching, the more reliably the waveform collapses toward its true form. Passive or dishonest observation reduces K-value and delays resolution.

Ley-paths: The ancient curved routes followed by the Wyrms through the Somerset landscape, aligned with water courses, mineral seams, and the invisible architecture of the Wyrd. The Fosse Way cut across these at right angles.

The Omega: The sum of all sums: the aggregate goodness that outlasts the decay of stone and bronze. Evil collapses to half its value; the Omega accumulates without limit, which is why the Winderwyrms won and will always win.

Superposition: The state of existing in more than one possible condition simultaneously, before a choice has been made and the waveform has collapsed. Farfrey existed in superposition before the first muffin was baked. Most of November exists in superposition.

Tharion: The ancient, Unphysical name for Somerset, used by the Wyrms before the Great Eagle arrived. Its etymology within the fiction relates to the covenants of Caelir The One. Its precise relationship to historical place-names is suggestive rather than literal.

Wumble-Chewing: The act of deliberating over a moral choice before the waveform collapses. Not procrastination, which is avoidance. Wumble-Chewing is active consideration with the full knowledge that a decision must eventually be made. The Winderwyrms do a great deal of it. The Snarleygogs do not do enough.

The Wyrd: Destiny or fate, as understood by the Anglo-Saxons and, in this cosmology, by the Winderwyrms who predate the Anglo-Saxons considerably. The Wyrd is not fixed but responsive; it moves through the Whisperflow and resonates in the Tor. Shakespeare's Weird Sisters are a mistranslation of the Wyrd Sisters, which is a different and more serious thing.

Appendix F: The Omega and the K-Value

The Omega represents the sum of all sums, the aggregate goodness that outlasts the decay of stone and bronze. In the Land of Farfrey the K-value, the efficiency score of moral observation, determines how quickly a waveform collapses into a stable form.

The fundamental law of Quantum Ethics operates as follows. Evil or ugly choices, such as the Snarleygog muffin, achieve initial value quickly. Their waveform collapses almost immediately into an impressive but ultimately unstable form.

The value of any evil choice at its peak is, by quantum ethical law, exactly half the value of the equivalent good choice at its peak. This is not a punishment. It is mathematics. The Snarleygog total, however they try, will always be half the Winderwyrm pile, and the Omega, which is the sum of all Winderwyrm piles across all time, cannot be reached by evil at all. It remains forever the shadow of what goodness approaches.

The K-value of the observer is not passive. A muffin baked in private, unobserved, still collapses its waveform, but the aggregate of honest moral observation accelerates the recognition of true value. The Winderwyrms' K-value, accrued across centuries of patient watching from the lichen-covered hills of Somerset, was considerable. Farfrey felt it.

Appendix G: Chronology of the Tharion Cycle

Before 43 AD: Gurt Wyrms and proto-Winderwyrms inhabit Tharion. The Daughters of Avalon maintain the library at the White Spring. The three ports of Buronium, Hinclaeth, and Paritonum trade in merry harmony. The silver lies undisturbed in the Mendip rock.

43 AD: Legio II Augusta arrives. Vespasian campaigns through the Southwest. The Mendip mines open within six years of the invasion. The Jinglewyrms begin to emerge from the fossil beds at Kelvenna.

50 to 350 AD: The Silver Alliance. Jinglewyrms accept the title of Custodes Litoris. Sacred springs are revealed. The Fosse Way is laid. The Ley-paths are cut. The ancient library at

Tor Velden is burned. Myrdda walks from Falmouth with salt in her hair and grief in her boots.

Approximate 350 to 380 AD: The Decree and the Slaying. The Gurt Wyrms issue the decree from the hollows of Shervage. The Jinglewyrms refuse. Three days of silence on the Somerset coast.

409 to 410 AD: Rome withdraws. The roads remain. The sandstone was always going to outlast the milestones.

Medieval period, date unstated: The Woodcutter's Error. It is not dated because it could have happened at almost any point between Rome's departure and the present, which is the point of it.

The present: The bracken stirs. The bluebells arrive without asking permission. Somewhere in Shervage Wood, a large fallen log smells faintly of wild garlic. In Farfrey, the Snarleygogs are learning to fold the eggs more carefully.

Appendix H: On the Wassailing Tradition and the Snarleygog Lament

The Waes-Hael Lament sung by the twelve Snarleygogs at Myrdda's transformation draws on the real Somerset tradition of wassailing: the midwinter ceremony of visiting orchards, singing to the trees, driving away evil spirits, and drinking cider in quantities that suggest the evil spirits put up considerable resistance. The word waes-hael is Old English, meaning be well, and the tradition is documented from at least the thirteenth century in Somerset and the west country, with earlier antecedents likely.

The wassail ceremony was about coaxing apple trees to produce a good harvest: encouraging a natural system to do what you needed it to do through a combination of ritual, noise, and the strategic application of cider to the roots. Encouraging Myrdda to produce a new identity and walk south to Cadbury under a name the king would not recognise is a more complex request, but the underlying principle is the same. The Snarleygogs as ritual practitioners is an unexpected detail. It is possible that their competitive intensity and their seventeen-chinned grumbling are not personality flaws but the natural properties of creatures who deal in transformations that are not easy and are not meant to be reversed. Good Queen Mira understood this. Myrdda, in becoming Myrddin, had no choice but to understand it also.

Appendix I: The Muffin as Moral Measure

The muffin is not an arbitrary choice. Bread-making is one of the oldest human technologies, one of the first acts by which early communities transformed raw material into something more nourishing than its components alone, and one of the few domestic processes that genuinely cannot be rushed without consequences. Bread will not rise faster because you want it to. The yeast works at its own rate. The dough requires its rest.

The muffin concentrates the entire moral question into a single domestic act. Every ingredient is a choice. Every choice carries a value. The aggregate of those values determines the outcome, and the outcome cannot be concealed: it either holds its dome or it does not.

The Snarleygog muffin is not merely a bad muffin. It is a demonstration that spite is an ingredient, that grudge changes the batter, that the desire to win faster than your opponent can be measured in the crumb structure of the result. The waveform collapses according to what was actually put in, not what was meant. The Omega Muffin, baked by all of Farfrey together, is not better because of any particular skill. It is better because nobody put spite in it. The absence of an ingredient is also a choice, and in quantum ethical terms it is among the most significant ones a baker can make.

PART OF THE HOLLOW VALE UNIVERSE

TWO BRITISH YULETYDE MYTHS FOR CHRISTMASSE TYME

POETRY OF THE FABLED GABLE OF ROMAN BRITAIN:

BY ALEXANDER PAUL BURTON

Book Preview: Whimsical Yuletide Poetry To Be Read Only When It Is December

Brother Faelric, The Monastery of St, Ambrose, Somerset, England, C. 608, Anno Domini

Without hesitation I share these tales, though I am reticent to show all of the translated Tharionese scrolls before they are properly and accurately translated. This Thursday last, I sat upon the crest of the hill overlooking the hilly glade which had been trampled on by a string of ponies; a fat lot of hungersome beasts who had wandered out from their barn at the farthest end of the pear orchard.

My heart briefly jolted at the sight of them out of the barn in the cold winter's night. Then, to my surprise, I reflected on the Lord's bounty and how all beings, however cold or needy, are provided for.

The short tales in this collection, including a preview of some other texts I have translated, is a taste of God's great kingdom in the time of Roman Britain, ere the coming of us Saxons some two hundred years, or centuries more, later.

Be bold in your reading of these tales. They do not seek to apologise for their languid use of prose and merry poetry. These are two short Yuletide tales for the more circumspect and wise amongst us all.

Brother Faelric, Somerset, England, Yuletide, 608 A.D.,

Perdix: A Partridge in a Pear Tree (Part One)

White Spring, Glastonbury (Hwit Fford, Tor Velden), Somerset (Tharion), C. 40 Anno Domini, During the Reign of Emperor Caligula, Before the Invasion of Britannia

The wind was blowing again. The green mists that emanated from the Whisperflow obscured the orchard's trees which once laden with fruit, now lay bare. Perdix was precariously crouched upon a rock with his claws digging into the damp stone; the only thing stopping him from falling were the small spiral runes which had been carved into them in ancient times. The wind still howled even now but had died down somewhat since the early morning mists had cleared, revealing a grey sky and pallid sun beneath a low, flat landscape. This vantage point was Perdix's favourite, and while he usually tended to stay on the top of Glastonbury Tor for many hours, today would be an exception as he had urgent business to attend to. He could not be late.

The Daughters of Avalon, as they were still called, had invited him to a special ceremony which was only to be held on the third night after the sun had stayed at its stillest. His ever observant nature had led him to conclude that this morning must be the third day, though he could only count by watching the languid leaves that remained on the orchard trees below. In their merry dance to the earth as occurred with the coming of the winter solstice, he noticed that some of the brown tendrils still held aloft small leaves which had not yet fallen. His beak clicked subtly as he watched the last leaf fall below him; a droplet of water fell from his bill and confirmed what he already knew: winter was a still season and even though the winds had not yet died down, there was still enough dampness in the morning air to confirm that this was indeed the winter solstice.

Perdix had not chosen to fly up the hillside after his brief breakfast, taken shortly after the morning moon had finally risen. He was a cautious fellow and preferred to use his wings only when in danger or in times where haste was needed over the slow footsteps of his gnarly claws. The climb to the top had taken an hour or two, which he measured by the rising of the sun and receding of the green mists and clouds which had slowly receded. A cloudy sky today; not snow or rain. Cloud. Perdix was confused by this as all the signs around him indicated that this was indeed the winter solstice. He noticed the holly bushes, the smell of ivy and even noticed the cherrywood smoke rising from the chimneys of humans who inhabited Street (Stratanhold), Catcott (Cattocum) and other small towns and hamlets around the Tor. He could not smell as clearly as the cunning fox or wolves that still roamed these parts, but he knew it was the deepest, darkest part of winter.

The ritual then began as the Daughters of Avalon were ready to bring the light of summer back into the oppressive bleakness that had enveloped the animals and human-beings of Britannia for far too long. The moon was at its brightest, but was slowly obscured by the dull radiance of the sun which was not yet fully revealed by the grey sky.

"We call on the Wyrd to guide us in our earthly works, which we seek to use to bring the light to the world of the living and un-Physical Hollow Vale's designs." Said Arch-Druid Brennus, a man of might and stature that Perdix respected deeply.

"Beseech thee, oh Danu. Oh Belisama. We are beholden to thee on this dark day of the coming of the light. Shelter us from evil. Keep us up high under the wings of your bounty and protection. Oh Danu. Oh Belisama." Responded an eager eyed apprentice who recited these words carefully. Perdix traced her lips and facial expressions carefully with his beady eyes, noting the changes in how her body moved and how her hands moved in unison with Brennus' hands.

As Perdix sat and watched he slowly fell into a trance. The ritual fire that burnt in the brazier next to the smooth stones began to change to a purple hue, emitting small sparks of light which made a soft "poof" sound as they exterminated any lingering mists. As the apprentice Maeve added more mistletoe and dried apple shards, the light grew more fierce and began to make a low humming sound as it matched the rhythm of the Tor beneath it.

His memory was not what it was, being over sixty years old made him forget his earliest and most profound memories. He supposed that Brennus and Maeve would consider him to be only four years old as he knew humans aged differently to him. Maeve had once communicated this to him in a deep-dream; they could not talk in the tongues of the physical Hollow Vale, but instead relied on the magick of the Star-born to communicate on high holidays.

As a sentinel of the land of this here western corner of Britannia, Perdix had taken his role very seriously. He was born in the year that many would term 36 A.D. in future times but he didn't work to the chronological timelines of human beings, preferring to observe the phases of the moon and seasons with his careful black eyes. A masculine ley-line and feminine ley-line intersected with a precision that coincided with the very same spot that he was born on. Hence his calling by Brennus, the Arch-Druid, to immerse his bountiful wisdom with that of the Wyrd's. He was to be guardian over not only his own brood, but also many creatures across the west-country: the brown robins in the orchards, the slippery adders that bask in the mid-summer sun, to other beastly spirits that lived in the water of the Whisperflow and dark pools amidst the bogs to the north of the Tor.

The curling smoke wafted over his red freckled chest, the greys and white dashes slowly disappearing as purple smoke enveloped his whole body. By now, Perdix was fully asleep in the deep-dream but was not yet responsive; this was the responsibility of Maeve who had not yet chanted the right incantation in Tharionese.

Byraeth spirareth, clymu saelon,
Toril æt nywl, wynthil ætern.
Aelfrun drithra, gemunan trym,
Wyrdaen hælenan, Perdix loyth.
Swefnunga wyrcan, bellum naedh,
Æt ende, ic hælde, saelon guardeth.

Breath of memory spirals, binding sight,
Hill in mist, veiled spirit eternal.
Old magic threads, remembering strength,
The Wyrd protects, Perdix loyal.
Dreams are made, the last bell calls,
At end, I hold, sight guards all.

A dream: ah, such bliss! Maeve had thrown the agèd partridge into a sweet dream of hues of blue and purple. In his long and forlorn life of trials and tribulations, the dear sentinel had not taken rest nor searched his own animalistic mind for the true purpose of his life. For if his brood had not yet seen their true purpose, that coming in years to come, the Wyrd saw true purpose in his actions and life. A steadfast keeper of the small beasts and spirits of the bogs and woodlands.

Caprice d'été Tra
Alexander Paul

Perdix: A Partridge in a Pear Tree (Part Two)

White Spring, Glastonbury (Hwit Fford, Tor Velden), Somerset (Tharion), C. 40 Anno Domini, During the Reign of Emperor Caligula, Before the Invasion of Britannia

His dream took him into the sky of purple velvet and piercing yellow stars. Perdix could not articulate it, but he was *of* the sky, not *in* the sky. He was part of the fabric of the sky and had been installed by Danu to protect the earthly realm of Tharion, or the west of Britannia, in timeless trust. The Gods willed it so. His corporeal body had vanished into feckless dust and feathers had turned to stars dotted into the glowing sky around him.

Then he saw it. A golden eagle adorned with the same hues of purple as the sky that held him and magick that had bore him hence. The eagle soared from the west, from far-off Italic Rome, carrying pledge and plight under both of her great wings. She flew against the ley-lines and through the mists, bemoaning her lot but mastering her task. She was to dominate Britannia in years to come, with men as her host and glory as her staff of wisdom. This was a conquering eagle, not of benevolent gold, but the kind that pillaged and burnt as it went.

His sadness deepened suddenly as a small white fox approached the Hwit Fford (White Spring of Glastonbury Tor), which in this age was not covered with a house of God but instead with the blindness of those who sought only spiritual hubris. The Daughters of Avalon had warned him of this: the fox would one day come for his brood and cherished family who had made this their abode.

As the white fox approached the stream, he could tell it was hungry. It sought something he could not ascertain, but found only whispers in the snow. This signalled transparency in the face of the test of loyalty; the Fox was not materially dangerous, only his will to dominate those around him. It approached the small nest on the north side of the White Spring (Hwit Fford) and approached carefully as the ignorant younglings slept in restful bliss; their slumber soon to be destroyed by the will of the ravenous white fox.

A sacrifice he did make from 'pon high. The purple stars embraced his pain and stars shone brighter than the light of the Star-born in their pity for Perdix. His family had been destroyed by this white fox; a spiritual beast of powerful hunger. He had gotten his fill and taken his leave. The nest was empty. The younglings were dead.

It was decided. Perdix's fate was decided. The fate of Britannia was deemed certain.

He fell out of the deep-dream and again felt the smothering purple smoke and ashen smell of mistletoe, ivy, bay and invoked herbs and plants. The mood had now hidden itself behind a shroud of piercing light that was brought forward by the coming of the mid-morning sun.

A trade was done in these moments. He would forgo an ordinary life of protection and loyalty to the present and look only to the future. His sacrifice to the white fox signalled the coming of an age of folly and might: the Roman Curse. His loyalty had been preserved through this sacrifice and would protect future sentinels, beasts and humans in the storm that was coming to the land of Britannia and Tharion.

In the coming years Perdix would be tested but his loyalty would never be questioned.

"To you I gift you the bough of the orchard's pear trees to reside in ever-more. The Wyrd wills you to use this to watch over the land." Maeve, the druid's apprentice, said to him as she bowed her head. A sign of respect in the world of beasts that fly.

Perdix didn't respond. He couldn't respond now that he was back in the physical realm. Instead, he bowed his small head in place of vocalised acquiescence. He kept it lowered until the druidic ritual had finished.

Mave carried on. "You shall make the White Spring (Hwti Fford) your abode forever more. On a lonesome bough on a lonesome pear tree shall you sit and watch as the golden eagle spreads its swarthy wings across these lands."

"Perdix the sentinel. Perdix the protector. Perdix of the Wyrd." Brennus confirmed in sombre silence, with a dry mouth and heart of hope, knowing that this silent sentinel would watch the land for years to come.

To Be Read If You Need Love's Protection

Perdix on his mound so green,
silent watching, silent seen.
He does spread his wings so far,
his brood protects by battle scar.

This our folly, this our pride
to sit above the storms we ride.
We seek not wisdom, only haste,
in God's protection that we do waste.

A brow upon the hill we sit,
the folly of our lives we flit.
Wasting gifts and His true love,
a silent yearning from above.

The bough we choose to spend our days,
we sit so blind, not in God's praise.
For love is boundless, endless wit,
seeking destiny, destiny's fit.

In goodly hand that flies above,
the lonesome silent, watching dove.
A hand of peace and silent jest,
to watch us blunder 'gainst His chest.

In life and love we serve ourselves,
but placed up high 'pon His shelves.
A welcome gesture, welcome home,
to seek the wing of Heaven's dome.

Caradoc and Brannoc: Two Turtle Doves

The Barge House, Hinkley Point (Hinclaeth), Somerset, England, 100 Anno Domini, During the Reign Emperor Trajan during peace-time in Britannia.

Barges flow from port to port,
A sailing blunder, in reeds caught.
Their clipped sterns and bows of reeds,
The wind that carries trusty steeds.

"'Arketh 'ere my Godly son. For I want to tell 'e a tale of when I did fail, this is a story told of thunder, in my younger days of youthful blunder." Caradoc murmured to his only son, Brannoc.

Before responding, he measured his father's temperament not by his tone, but by the number of clay cider pots that lay strewn across the quiet room. He moved closer to his father, the smoke in the room making his presence more intimate and visceral than his usual interactions. "Yes, father. I am listening."

"Have you heard of the tale of the two doves of ancient Tharion?" he asked, using only half of his mouth as he smoked his pipe of mugwort and heather-weed, making a small plume of smoke rise suddenly without warning in thin blue-grey wisps. This weed was often called Myrvail-Hyrthana in Tharionesese vernacular. It was a blend of plants that provided a dream-like feeling in the user. It was common across the land and often smoked by those who were elders in their hamlets or communities as a way of channelling wisdom.

"I heard that the doves do not exist. They did not exist. Only in dreams did they exist. It is the ports of Buronium, Hinclaeth and Paritonum (Bridgwater), all three combined which form the myth. Surely it is only a myth for children?"

"'Tis so my son. But there is more to this tale. For you named three ports. Three is not a number that makes the Gods pleased. Danu, in her wisdom, contrived another ending to this tale." He took another drag of the weed, then closed his eyes and rhythmically nodded his head back and forth in a way that showed his mind was delving deep into the mists of time.

He interrupted his father's meditative state carefully. "I see. I see. But father, why three ports and only two doves?"

His brow crumpled slightly as his eyes moved closer toward the centre of his eyes, focussing narrowly on Brannoc in a way that made him nervous. His father was searching deep within his very being to ascertain the true meaning of the question. Caradoc perhaps found his question somewhat perplexing in his current state. "They fought."

He paused, taking in the gravitas of how his father had said the sentence with such ardour, as if the answer was obvious enough to reveal the significance. "They fought? And the Doves died? What do you mean?"

Before answering, his father reclined slightly in his chair, adjusting his knees and feet to make himself more comfortable as he relit his Myrvail-Hyrthana pipe. He struggled to light it for a few seconds but eventually continued to give Brannoc an answer. "In the days before these here Romans blighted our land of Tharion, an ancient Trinity of trade existed in merry harmony upon our northern shores: Buronium, Hinclaeth and Paritonum."

Brannoc nodded. He knew this. "But father, I know this."

His father continued, ignoring his interjection. "The people of Paritonum broke their agreement and fought on the side of the Romans when they invaded. They chose gold over kin, forsaking their Arthon heritage and that of the Star-born."

"What did they do?"

"They traded fragments of the Star-Ark and stone tablets of the Arthons, which were brought here hence nearly two and half thousand years ago by Mira, the First-Born of Tharion. They opened the Star-Vault and emptied it in exchange for salt trading privileges in all of Tharion and the west-country."

"They traded raw magick for trade exclusivity? But Danu would punish them, surely?"

His father nodded. "Danu surely did, and invoked the wrack of Luna. For she is a jealous moon and jealous of the earth in its temporal fecklessness."

"What did they do, father? The Gods I mean..." Brannoc asked, astounded by the stupidity of the merchants of Paritonum.

"Thanks to their treason, with blood on their hands, the river fell silent. The Whisperflow stopped bringing currents of the Wyrd to The Bell. It made no sound and stopped flowing to Avalonae. The White Stream fell silent, too. Tor Velden and the Knoll of Horns stopped harmonious resonance with the Wyrd."

“Why did the silence befall those places?”

His father answered after a brief pause. “

“But what of the merchants? And the Doves?” He said this eagerly as he tried to decode the rest of what his father had explained. There were so many pieces to try to fit together in his mind.

“There were no doves. At least, no more doves to be seen ever again in Paritonum. The marshes fell silent and the dearth of their treason blackened the very bogs of Hinclaeth and turned the wells of Buronium to brine.”

Before explaining the Doves, Caradoc stopped and relit his pipe. He continued. “The souls of the two ports abandoned the spiral of time out of grief. Two Turtle Doves met one Sunday after the treason and never returned. In their sadness, they flew west across the great sea, never to be seen again. They were stricken with doubt and broken of heart, never to return to the shores of Britannia.”

“... And that’s why we celebrate them? For their loyalty, I mean.”

“Yes, son. That is why.” His father bowed his head as he said this, saddened at the tale of broken partnership, broken loyalty and grief turned to regret. “The Doves were a sign of undying loyalty and steadfast conviction. They were the Old and the New. They were outside the Wyrd and spiral of time.”

Thus it was known for eternity: the tale of the two doves,

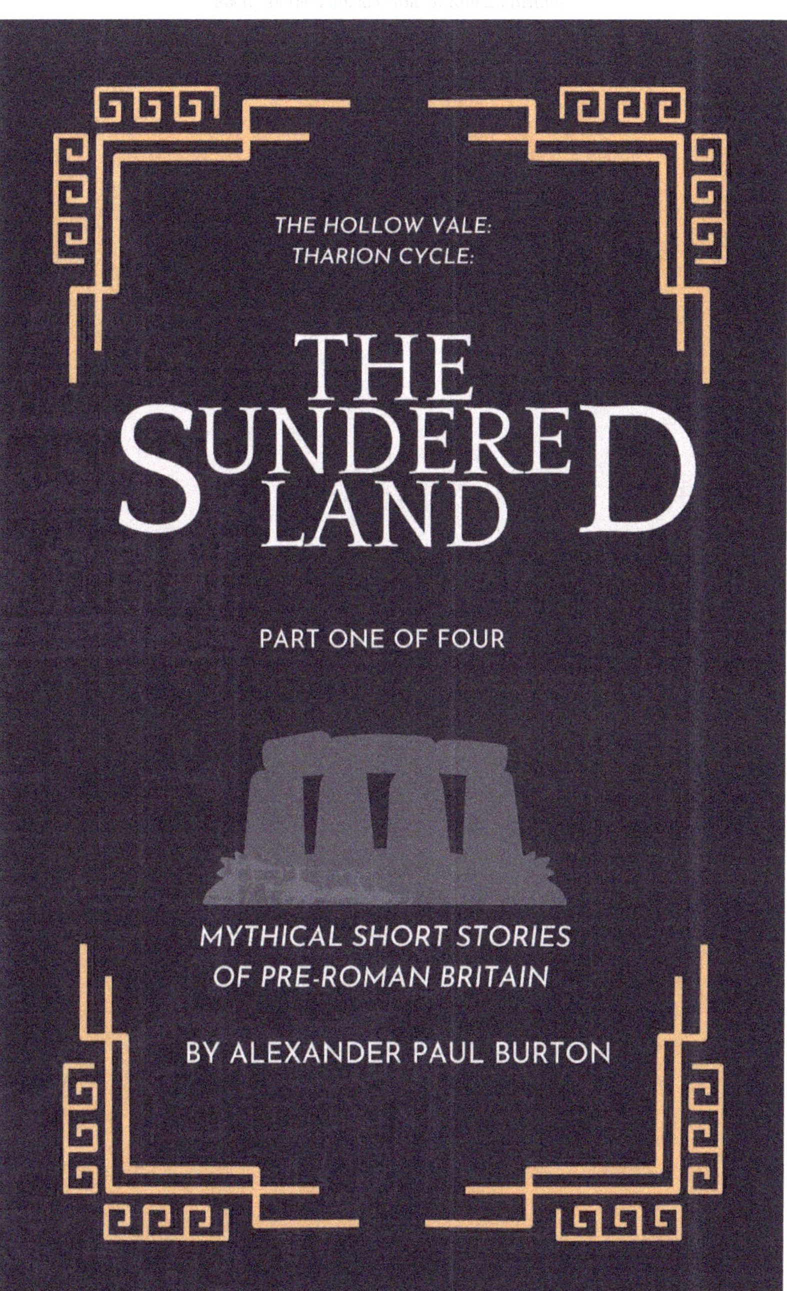

THE HOLLOW VALE:
THARION CYCLE:

THE SUNDERED LAND

PART ONE OF FOUR

MYTHICAL SHORT STORIES
OF PRE-ROMAN BRITAIN

BY ALEXANDER PAUL BURTON

Book preview: The Sundered Land

Mythical Short Stories of Pre-Roman Britain
Part One of Four

By Alexander Paul Burton

Chapter I: The First Song

Sahara Desert, Saelhara, North Africa, Circa 2500 BC, Neolithic/Early Bronze Age, The Reign of Mamun, Defender of The Heavenly Arthons, Before The Coming Of The Storm.

> *"A small boat of wattle and wisp*
> *crept into the that fleeting mist*
> *and as the sunrise tore the clouds,*
> *Mira sat under blue shrouds.*
>
> *She pondered where she'd go that day,*
> *the river Tem'se's at low tide's sway,*
> *a longer route than land or air,*
> *Mira sat with hazel hair.*
>
> *A pallid scornful night before,*
> *had sent her rage with storms in store,*
> *a rain that soaked her very bones,*
> *Mira-prophet reading tomes. "*

Mira scratched a poem and prose into a small wax tablet she kept in her hemp satchel. She paused after the last sentence and stopped before she entirely lost control of the boat. The water spread as thin as ice and as still as winter's silent nights as it spread from the stern of the small white ship into the distant horizon. A brown tendril of bruised rope spread languidly beside the boat, strewn across the still water. A pale sunrise reached over the low brown woodland in the distance. The damp smell of hemp hit Mira's nose and the gentle breeze sent particles of damp seawater into each of her nostrils, down into her lungs. This augmented the slightly rotting goat hide that covered the lower side of the small craft. She shook her head to wake herself up as she narrowed her eyes to see further ahead. She could clearly see into the distance and saw the oncoming land mass with clarity. Smooth were the harsh sounds of three white birds in the sky. Their wings spread out and flapped lazily as they zig-zagged and briefly blocked the sun. A shadow fell on her forehead and lower chin as she wiped the sea-mist from her brow. She had not set out in vain, for though she had left in haste without a great store of provisions or blessings, the fact remained that she had reached the land that her father had told her about three days prior, before the coming of the rain.

Her father Mamun had been guided by a seven-pointed star the colour of lapis only seven days before her own great journey; a mere four days before the coming of the rain. The folk of the enclosed hamlet had remarked that he was blessed by the wisdom of Caelir The One, who had sent it as a gift to guide him in future times of strife. Upon hearing his great news from the seven-pointed star, he waited four days and then laid down all of his gold and great wealth and paid for a feast of victuals, aloe mead and music to play at such a merry temperament that all in attendance from site round yonder did make cheery sounds and dance through the night. Oh, what a Godly sight! A great time of mirth for all, both beast and man. Many then remembered and kept in memory such happy hours before the storm of Anghar. After Mamun's feast, the rain raged for three nights until the very reeds were wet with the folly of the anger of Caelir The One. This was not a storm of tears or anger. No, these were storms of mirth. These were storms of plenty and grace sent from the heavens in their purple hued celestial throne that spirals from End to End. Caelir, a silent sentinel sitting high, watching in quiet repose in purple fecklessness.

The gift of wetness and rain that they bore hence to this goodly earthen seat, upon the temporal orb, fell on a bed of grass and trees. It was thunderous in sound. The rain and angry showers of plenty fell in a rapid rush/ This pleased the crops that had dried from drought before. Many months of sun had brought the farmers' crops wholly to hues of grey and pale dust. They had been a shadow of their former bounty, now lost to the fearsome might of the ever-trying progress of entropy; the movement of time and probabilistic conclusion that all living things must change, and not always for the best. For months the people who followed Mamun had waited for Caelir The One to send news from heaven's purple sky. A majestic realm that lay above in peaceful rest and relative quiet; Caelir's sky.

The gift was intended to be celebrated by all who lived on those green mounds. But from atop their mounds they saw not a future that graced their eyes with hope. Instead, Mamun's people felt a fleeting sadness, they groped and searched around for reasons to explain this endless rain. It surely had to end, for the wetness that fell plundered the very happiness they thought they had welcomed, the very happiness they had sought for years during many seasons of drought.

Some sought to escape the gift of rain, for they wanted to live in new lands. Those same hands pointed north-west, but they gained no recognition for their prophecy. These prophets, known as the Heavenly Arthons, had waited years for this rain. Many years they had waited, recording the spiral turning of the entropic sky on their tablets each passing sun and passing moon. On tablets and tomes the Arthons scratched a simple 'T' rune for the passing of the celestial fire, Sol, who is the sun, and an 'O' rune for the passing of the Luna, a blight in the sky for her circular celestial disappointment.

The Arthons rumoured that in Luna's scorn for the creation of the earth, she was down-graded and whittled by

Caelir The One himself and made to become evermore a mere moon and no longer a mighty monolith in the purple celestial realm. Luna was made a moon in her own right, being punished for her haughty jealousy thus remaining evermore not a planet.

The Arthon's counted countless nights and wrote the runes when the sun shone in His dangling might. In brilliant photonic light, Sol was strewn across the firmament and thus called the 'mid-day sun' who thusly agreed to flash his cosmic ray to radiate and heat. This heat made the clouds cry with rain for three days. The showers of blues and hues of purple-grey set ablaze the sky with the colours of newness, so graceful were those drops of life-giving water In this respect, the temporal earth was to become a receptacle of the goodness of the divine. The water was formed and scattered to replenish the land, sea and dryness of old. Wetness, or disorder, is the true source of creation, of inspiration and sets in severe repose against a dry world of static material non–divinity.

Before the coming of the rain, Mamun had directed the people of the enclosed hamlet to find every pot, receptacle and jar they held in their goodly homes. The seven-pointed star had directed him to not bring force or will power against the coming deluge.

For this deluge was a gift, and no gift of Caelir The One must be horded. All pots, receptacles and canisters were to be smashed and burnt as an offering.

A treasonous pact was made: that if a person should fight the will of any single drop of water, that if it be held by human willpower, it would be as if Caelir's very own will had been challenged. The water must run. The flood would run its course and the deluge would smother the Arthon's land in newness and chaos: a delight of the heavens and creation itself.

All the people and folk from far did bring their pots, jars and clay urns to Mamun's great feast. A fire they created and smashed, crashed and burnt all receptacles.

Now available on all platforms. Check my author profile or visit
www.alexanderpaulburton.com

Caprice d'été Trois
Alexander Paul

About the Author

Alexander Paul Burton is a storyteller, composer, and quiet mapmaker of memory. Born in Britain and shaped by the hills, marshes, and merry lanes of Cornwall and Somerset, he grew up not with myths, but among them. His earliest influences were not dragons or swords, but the forgotten names on mile-markers, the ghosts in railway timetables, and the way mist clings to stone like something remembering itself.

Now based in Toronto, Alexander continues to write across fictitious history and imagination. His fiction and music explore the borderlands between place and presence, between what is lost and what remains. He draws inspiration from etymology, folklore, and the small, resonant silences between people. His background in nonprofit and public sector work has shaped a lifelong belief: that stories are vessels, for grief, for joy, for remembering differently.

His writing is steeped in the language of echoes, *vethir anneth*, the unspoken truths that dwell in silence, and guided by the mantra of the Daughters of Avalon: *ethra scripen vanna*, what is written in resonance, echoes in the soul.

Alexander Paul Burton, Toronto, Ontario

https://www.alexanderpaulburton.com/the-hollow-vale-wiki

www.ingramcontent.com/pod-product-compliance
Lightning Source LLC
Chambersburg PA
CBHW072304130726
47910CB00012B/2429